OTHER FIVE STAR NOVELS
BY ETHAN J. WOLFE

MYSTERY NOVELS AS AL LAMANDA

Sunset (nominated for the Edgar Award)
Sunrise (winner of the 2014 best crime novel)
First Light (nominated for the Nero Award)
This Side of Midnight (nominated for the Nero Award)
With Six You Get Wally (Winner of the Nero Award))

WESTERN NOVELS AS ETHAN J. WOLFE

The Last Ride
The Regulator
The Range War of '82
Murphy's Law
All The Queen's Men
One if by Land
The Cattle Drive
The Devil's Waltz
Comanche Sunrise
The Reckoning
Lawman
Baker's Dozen
The Horse Soldier
The Illinois Detective Agency: The Case of the Missing Cattle
The Illinois Detective Agency: The Case of the Stalking Moon
The Illinois Detective Agency: The Case of Duffy's Revenge

MURPHY'S REVENGE

AL LAMANDA, WRITING AS ETHAN J. WOLFE

FIVE STAR

A part of Gale, a Cengage Company

GALE
A Cengage Company

LIBRARY OF CONGRESS CATALOGING-IN-PUBLICATION DATA

Names: Wolfe, Ethan J., author.
Title: Murphy's revenge / Al Lamanda, writing as Ethan J. Wolfe.
Description: First Edition. | Waterville, Maine : Five Star, a part of Gale, a Cengage Company, 2023. | Series: The Regulator series ; book 7 |
Identifiers: LCCN 2022022680 | ISBN 9781432895648 (hardcover)
Subjects: LCGFT: Detective and mystery fiction. | Novels.
Classification: LCC PS3612.A5433 M88 2023 | DDC 813/.6—dc23
LC record available at https://lccn.loc.gov/2022022680

First Edition. First Printing: January 2023
Find us on Facebook—https://www.facebook.com/FiveStarCengage
Visit our website—http://www.gale.cengage.com/fivestar
Contact Five Star Publishing at FiveStar@cengage.com

Printed in Mexico
Print Number: 1   Print Year: 2023

MURPHY'S REVENGE

CHAPTER ONE

Kai, Murphy's wife of eighteen months, hung wash on the line beside the house he had built ten miles south of Fort Smith, Arkansas. The land was rich, and a stream ran through the property, allowing for an indoor and outdoor pump for fresh water.

Their adopted daughter, Aideen, named for Murphy's mother, watched from the crib Murphy had built where an old stump once sat in the ground. Murphy was as stubborn as he was handy. He could have hitched a team to pull the stump from the ground, but instead he spent countless hours chopping away at it with an ax until nothing remained but a hole in the ground that he filled in.

Kai was a mixture of Navajo, Sioux, Irish, and English. She was as tall as or taller than the average man of the day, slim and muscular. She was a very capable person and knew the ways of the Navajo and Sioux as well as those of her white ancestors. In addition to English, she spoke Navajo, Sioux, and French, which she'd learned from missionaries.

When school was in session, Kai taught on the reservation in the Indian Nation in the Ozarks.

When school was in recess, Murphy moved them to his farm in Tennessee. The farm grew corn, which was shipped to his father's farm nearby for the purpose of making bourbon whiskey.

Michael Murphy started making bourbon forty years earlier and produced around four hundred barrels a year of the agedin-the-keg sipping whiskey. He didn't bottle it, but sold the kegs to various companies to brand. He kept a reserve to bottle for family and local merchants for saloons.

Kai turned her head when Murphy stepped onto the porch. He wore his black trail clothes and black-handled Colt revolver. Saddlebags hung over his left shoulder. He held a Winchester rifle in his right hand.

He stepped off the porch, walked to her, and kissed Kai on the neck.

"How long will you be gone?" Kai said.

"A week," Murphy said.

Kai looked up at Murphy. He stood six-foot-four in his stocking feet; inches taller when wearing his boots. As hard as he was to those who crossed his path, Murphy was equally gentle with her and the baby.

"Don't dawdle. We have work to do," Kai said.

"Yes, ma'am," Murphy said.

He went to the barn for his horse, Boyle.

Aideen appeared on the porch and then walked down to Kai. "You should come to the farm for a few weeks," Aideen said.

In her early sixties, Aideen was a handsome, no-nonsense woman who was always cheerful and cordial, unless you got her dander up. She was very much like Kai in that regard.

"He'll be back in a week," Kai said. "We'll go south when the weather turns."

Murphy walked Boyle out of the barn. Boyle was an exceptionally large horse Murphy had raised from a colt.

"You have other horses, son. Why not give Boyle a rest?" Aideen said.

"He'd never forgive me if I rode another horse," Murphy said.

Kai lifted the baby from the crib. Murphy kissed Kai, the baby, and Aideen.

8

"Mother, you'll stay until I return?" Murphy said.

"Of course," Aideen said. "Now go on with you. We have work to do."

Murphy mounted the saddle, tipped his black Stetson to Kai and Aideen, and then rode Boyle through the gate in the picket fence.

"We're low on supplies," Aideen said.

"I'll hitch the buggy after I'm done with the wash," Kai said. "We'll take a ride into town."

"Let's have lunch in town," Aideen said.

"All right," Kai said.

Kai parked the buggy in front of the large general store on Front Street. She put the brake on, then climbed down and took the baby from Aideen. Then Aideen stepped down and, together with Kai, they entered the general store.

Mr. Greenly, the owner of the general store, greeted Kai with a "Good afternoon, Mrs. Murphy," and a smile.

Before she met and married Murphy, Kai wasn't exactly welcome in most circles. She was considered a half-breed and a squaw, a woman who had lived with the savages. She'd married a US Marshal a decade earlier and, after he was murdered by outlaws, she converted their home into a boardinghouse to make ends meet.

It was chance, or luck, or fate, that brought Murphy to her boardinghouse one night when he was on a mission for the president. They developed a friendship that blossomed into romance and led to marriage.

Since her marriage to Murphy, Kai found herself in popular demand in society circles. Doors normally closed to her were opened overnight.

She had no illusions as to the reasons for her elevated status. Murphy was the most feared man she had ever met, and his ferocious persona translated to respect for his wife—or be prepared for the consequences.

Some folks were genuine in their treatment of her. Judge Parker held her in high regard and had even appointed her a teacher on the reservation. Murphy's parents loved her and treated her as a daughter.

Most people found it easier to be nice to her in public rather than deal with Murphy's fearsome temper.

After placing an order with Mr. Greenly, Kai and Aideen and the baby walked to Main Street to have lunch at Delmonico's Restaurant.

"Aideen, would you mind if I stopped to see Judge Parker for a moment?" Kai said after lunch.

"No, dear, but I'll stay with the baby in the carriage," Aideen said.

Judge Parker was in his chambers when Kai was escorted in to see him. Parker wasn't fifty years old but appeared older due to his white hair and beard. He was Kai's height and wore a crisp suit. Despite his reputation as "the hanging judge," he was quite soft spoken.

"Kai, I wasn't expecting you in town for a while yet," Parker said. "I hope you're not angry with me for borrowing your husband."

Kai smiled. "No, Judge, of course not," she said. "I wanted to talk to you about the school."

"You've been doing a wonderful job, Kai. I hope nothing is wrong," Parker said.

"Everything is fine," Kai said. "I would like to teach music to the children. I can read and write music, but I can't play an instrument. Can you recruit some musicians who might be willing to donate their time?"

Parker nodded his head as he thought. "I think I might," he

said. "I'll have them report here and send for you to speak with them."

"Thank you, Judge," Kai said.

"How is the baby?"

"Just fine. She's downstairs with Aideen," Kai said.

"Tell Mrs. Murphy I sent my regards," Parker said.

"I will."

As Kai climbed into the wagon, Aideen said, "Before we leave town let's have the doctor check the baby."

"Is she sick?" Kai said.

"No, but a checkup can't hurt anything."

"All right," Kai said.

Doctor Brewster was one of two doctors in Fort Smith. He was in his sixties and had been practicing medicine for thirty-five years. He examined the baby thoroughly and pronounced her to be very fit and healthy.

"How is Mr. Murphy, Kai?" Brewster said. "Last I saw him, I took a bullet out of his shoulder and he was pretty beat up."

"A week after you patched him up he was chopping wood and building a corral," Kai said.

"Well, tell him I said hello," Brewster said.

After supper, Kai and Aideen took coffee on the front porch and watched the sky darken.

"She'll sleep for a while," Aideen said. "I'll get the first feeding."

"Murphy's been doing that," Kai said. "First and last feeding."

"My son?" Aideen said. "Are we talking about the same man?"

"You'd be surprised how gentle he can be when he wants to be," Kai said.

"How about some more coffee while it's still hot?" Aideen said.

Kai nodded. Aideen went inside and returned with the pot and a bottle of her husband's whiskey. She filled the cups and then opened the whiskey bottle and splashed in an ounce.

"What would Michael say?" Kai said.

"Nothing, dear," Aideen said. "A woman doesn't always tell her husband everything, now does she?"

Kai grinned and then took a sip from her cup. "Good stuff," she said.

"Yes," Aideen said. "Yes it is."

CHAPTER TWO

William Burke's office was located in the basement of the White House. To be honest, it was more like hidden in the basement of the White House.

Burke had worked for three presidents now, going back to Grant. He held no official title, yet carried more power than anyone else on the president's staff. He never voted in an election. He didn't want to appear biased.

What Burke did for the presidents was remove problems from their path using any means possible. His reports were never read by anyone but the president, and never discussed outside the Oval Office.

Burke was nearing sixty and didn't know how many more years he had to serve, but he was growing weary of the Washington shuffle and was looking forward to the day he could retire.

He was writing a report at his desk when an aide to President Chester Arthur told him the president requested his presence in the Oval Office.

Burke tossed on his suit jacket and took the stairs to the Oval Office.

Arthur was at his desk when Burke entered the office.

"You sent for me, sir?" Burke said.

"Come in, Bill," Arthur said.

Burke took a chair facing the desk.

"As you know, I won't be seeking a second term due to my

13

poor health," Arthur said.

"And how are you feeling, sir?" Burke said.

"Good and bad days, Bill," Arthur said.

"Yes sir," Burke said.

"The front-runner to win the election is the governor of New York, Grover Cleveland," Arthur said.

"I've heard that," Burke said.

"We may be of different political parties, but Cleveland is a good man," Arthur said. "He will be stumping for six weeks and will need a security detail. I recommended Murphy to head it up."

"Murphy?" Burke said.

"I know, I know. After his last assignment the man won't even speak to me," Arthur said.

"Don't take offense to that, sir. Murphy hardly speaks to anybody," Burke said.

"He'll speak to you," Arthur said.

Burke sighed.

"I am still the president for eight more months; I can order him to take the assignment," Arthur said.

"I'll send him a telegram," Burke said.

"Go in person," Arthur said.

"Yes sir," Burke said.

"Take this file on Cleveland with you," Arthur said. "And don't let Murphy bully you. I'll send troops down there and bring him back under arrest."

Burke nodded. "I'll go home and pack," he said.

As he packed a large suitcase, Burke sipped from a glass of whiskey and smoked a cigar. This was a trip he didn't wish to make.

Murphy had served his country for a very long time. As an officer for the Union Army during the Civil War. As a secret service agent for President Grant. As a Regulator for Grant and every president since.

For God and country, Murphy has served and killed many men.

Now all he wanted to do was live quietly with Kai and their new baby girl and leave everything else behind him.

Burke drained his glass and poured another.

"What are you worried about, Bill?" he said aloud. "He'll probably shoot you on sight. And if he doesn't, Kai will."

CHAPTER THREE

Kai and Aideen were working in the vegetable garden, hoeing the ground to get ready for planting seeds.

On the porch, the baby slept in her basket.

Aideen noticed a cloud of dust on the road and said, "Someone is coming."

Kai cupped her hands and looked down the road. "Son of a bitch," she said.

"Kai, your language," Aideen said.

Kai ran into the house. Aideen followed her to the porch and checked on the baby. Kai emerged with a shotgun.

"What in the world?" Aideen said.

Kai descended the steps and ran to the open gate. The baby woke up and cried, and Aideen took her in her arms, then joined Kai.

"Come on, you son of a bitch. Keep coming," Kai said.

"Kai, what is . . . ?" Aideen said.

"Burke," Kai said.

"Oh, no," Aideen said.

"Yeah," Kai said.

"Son of a bitch," Aideen said.

Kai grinned. "Exactly right," she said.

Burke arrived in his rented buggy and stopped at the gate.

"Turn around and go home, Mr. Burke," Kai said. "You're not welcome here."

"Where is he, Kai?" Burke said.

Kai cocked both barrels of the shotgun. "I won't ask you to leave again," she said.

"I'm here by order of President Arthur," Burke said. "We both know I can't leave without seeing Murphy."

Kai sighed and lowered the shotgun.

"I'll make some coffee," Aideen said.

Burke, Kai, and Aideen sat in chairs on the porch with cups of coffee. Burke smoked a cigar.

"How are things, Kai?" Burke said.

"Why can't you people leave him alone?" Kai said. "Hasn't he been shot enough for you, or are you determined to see him killed?"

"This is a very simple assignment, Kai," Burke said.

"They all are until he gets shot or stabbed or stranded in a desert and comes limping home half dead," Kai said.

"Governor Cleveland of New York is running for president," Burke said. "He will be on a six-week stumping tour. President Arthur wants Murphy to head up the security detail."

Kai glared at Burke.

"I know what you're thinking," he said. "It won't be like that."

"They never are, are they?" Kai said.

"Kai, we both know he's going to do this, so why don't you tell me where he is and save us both a lot of bickering," Burke said.

"He went to the Indian Nation in the Ozarks to do a favor for Judge Parker," Kai said. "He'll be gone a week."

"I see," Burke said.

"Mr. Burke, look around you," Aideen said. "My son is married with a young baby to care for. Every time you call, his life is at risk. When is enough, enough?"

"I wish I had an answer for you, Mrs. Murphy," Burke said.

"When he's dead, that's when you'll be satisfied," Kai said.

"I guess I'll ride back to town and get a hotel room," Burke said.

"Well, you're bloody well not staying here," Kai said.

After dinner, Kai and Aideen took coffee on the porch and watched the night sky reveal the stars.

"If he's going to New York, I suggest we go with him and have a visit with President Grant," Kai said.

"Both of us?" Aideen said.

"Why not?" Kai said.

"My son will . . ." Aideen said.

"Make him think it's his own idea and he'll agree," Kai said. "That's how you deal with your son."

"You have learned to think like a woman," Aideen said.

"More like a wife," Kai said.

Aideen and Kai looked at each other and laughed.

CHAPTER FOUR

In the morning, Burke took coffee on the balcony of his hotel room facing Main Street. In the background, the massive courthouse dominated the scenery.

Along with coffee, he ordered two slices of buttered toast, his usual breakfast. Lunch was a bit more substantial and dinner even more so, but he liked to eat light in the morning.

As he munched toast and sipped coffee, he composed the telegram he would send to the president. He ordered a bath for ten o'clock. As soon as he finished toast and coffee, he changed into a robe and went down the hall to the bathing room.

As he soaked in the tub, Burke lit a cigar. He happened to agree with Kai that enough was enough concerning Murphy. The man had handled countless assignments for three presidents, and in the course of his duties, killed an untold number of men.

Murphy had more scars on his body than any man had a right to bear.

Yet, here he was, hat in hand, asking Murphy to fulfill one more assignment. In a strange way, Burke felt shame.

Judge Parker received Burke in his chambers.

"Have a seat," Parker said as he poured coffee for Burke.

Burke took a chair facing the desk.

"I can only assume you're here to see Murphy," Parker said.

"The president has an assignment for him," Burke said.

"I figured that the moment they told me you were here," Parker said.

Burke took a sip of coffee. "I've already been lectured by Kai and his mother about leaving him alone, so I'm aware of how everybody feels, me included."

"You?" Parker said.

"I think Murphy has done enough for his country, don't you?" Burke said.

"I'm afraid I have to agree," Parker said.

"Yet he is on assignment for you right now," Burke said.

"A small favor," Parker said. "A week at most."

"I have some telegrams to send," Burke said. "How about having lunch with me at my hotel?"

"One o'clock?" Parker said. "I have several cases I need to pass judgment on at three."

"One o'clock," Burke said.

After leaving Parker, Burke walked to the telegraph office and sent a telegram to Arthur, informing him he would be in Fort Smith for a week, awaiting Murphy's return.

Having nothing else to do, Burke took a walk around Fort Smith. The changes since the war were amazing, to say the least. A town of less than a thousand before the war, it now boasted some five thousand residents.

Burke, assigned to General Steele, had spent a year in Fort Smith when Steele's army took control of the town from the Confederates.

Now Fort Smith had shops, stores, private homes, churches, the courthouse, and even a small college.

In addition to presiding over the court system for most of Arkansas, Judge Parker had full authority over the Indian Nation in the Ozarks.

Although Parker had no real authority over Murphy, the fact that Murphy agreed to take an assignment from the judge meant

Murphy held Parker in high regard.

Burke stopped in a tobacco shop and purchased a dozen Cuban cigars. When he reached his hotel, he sat on the porch with a cup of coffee and smoked a cigar.

Thoughts of retirement entered his mind. Maybe it was time for him to quit the Washington game and settle somewhere and live out his days quietly. He had enough money saved to last three lifetimes, so that was no worry.

He was weary of political games and of having to use men like Murphy. Those in power and in the big cities back east believed the country to be civilized and refined. They had no understanding of the west and how dangerous a place it really was.

At twelve-thirty, Burke went to his room to freshen up. He changed his shirt and then met Parker for lunch.

CHAPTER FIVE

The ride to Belle Starr's hideaway cabin in the Ozark Mountains took nearly three days. Murphy had been there before and knew the way. Indian scouts would be out along the way, but they wouldn't show themselves unless he gave them reason.

If he shot a deer, that would bring a party of twenty to his camp. A rabbit would go unnoticed. The land was rich with game and water, so there was no need to kill a deer, and that rule was generally observed by whites crossing the reservation.

As he ate a breakfast of eggs, bacon, and biscuits, Murphy kept his wits about him. The five tribes, consisting of Cherokee, Choctaw, Muscogee, Chickasaw, and Seminole, were all on friendly terms, to each other and the white man, but respect was demanded and expected.

They were used to white traders visiting. The Indian Affairs people and even Judge Parker would visit on occasion. They knew Kai well, as their schoolteacher and a friend. They knew Murphy as her husband and as a lawman. They knew Murphy as a fierce but fair warrior and as a man of honor.

The reservation had its own police force. The police were selected by the chiefs for their courage and honesty. The reservation had its own laws and punishments for breaking them, and Judge Parker never interfered unless federal law was violated by a tribe member off the reservation. In such a case, Parker would send Marshal Bass Reeves to investigate.

Reeves was born a slave, escaped during the war, and lived

with the Cherokee for nearly ten years. He was a member of the tribe, and his word was well respected.

As he drank coffee and smoked his pipe, Murphy watched a lone rider approach his camp. He wore the clothing of a reservation police officer. His horse was saddled, and he carried a rifle as well as a sidearm. A reservation police badge was pinned to his vest.

His name was Joseph Black Fox, and he was Cherokee.

At the camp, Joseph nodded and dismounted.

"Want some coffee?" Murphy said.

"I could use some," Joseph said.

Murphy filled a cup with coffee and handed it to Joseph, who sat beside the fire.

"What brings you this far?" Murphy said.

"Some stupid kid stole a horse to impress a woman and got caught," Joseph said. "He ran away and is hiding in the mountains."

"He's hiding a half day's ride south in an old prospector's cabin," Murphy said. "I passed him yesterday afternoon. He didn't know I spotted him."

"I know the cabin," Joseph said. "Thanks."

"Try a hunk of that cornbread. Kai baked it," Murphy said.

Joseph took a slice. "My son thinks he is going to marry her when he is of age," he said.

"She's his teacher," Murphy said.

Joseph nodded. "I told him grown women don't marry nine-year-old boys, especially when they are already married," he said.

Murphy grinned. "I think they call that puppy love," he said.

"Puppy love?" Joseph said. "I will remember that. So why are you here?"

"Judge Parker asked me to deliver a message to Belle Starr," Murphy said.

"Why didn't he send Reeves or the one with the eye patch?" Joseph said.

"I've had dealings with her before," Murphy said. "She'll be less likely to shoot and more likely to listen to me than to other people."

"Well, I'd better head to the cabin," Joseph said. "Thanks for the coffee."

After Joseph left, Murphy broke camp and headed to Belle Starr's cabin. He would be there by noon. It was located on the Oklahoma side of the Ozarks and off the reservation land.

The ride ascended as he neared the cabin. The last five hundred feet, Murphy had to dismount, as it was too steep a pitch for horse and rider. He walked Boyle to the top. He could have taken a back door pass, but that added two days to the trip.

As he reached the top of the mountain, Murphy saw smoke coming from the chimney of the cabin. He walked Boyle toward the corral where just a few horses were housed.

Belle Starr in all her glory came out of the cabin and stood on the porch, holding a cocked shotgun aimed at Murphy.

The sun was at Murphy's back and Belle had to squint to see who it was. Then she said, "Murphy, you son of a bitch, have you come to arrest me again?"

"I bring you a message from Judge Parker," Murphy said.

"Come ahead," Belle said as she set the shotgun aside.

Murphy tied Boyle to the hitching post and climbed the steps to the stairs.

"Got a fresh pot on the stove," Belle said and went inside.

Murphy took a chair. Belle returned with two cups and gave him one, then sat beside him.

"I thought maybe you was holding a grudge for those shenanigans last year," Belle said.

"You know better than that," Murphy said.

"I expect so," Belle said. "So what's this message?"

Murphy reached into his shirt pocket for the folded document and handed it to Belle. She unfolded it and read it quickly.

"This says Parker is willing to give me amnesty if I swear to him to give up my outlaw ways," Belle said.

"He means it, Belle," Murphy said. "Pack up supplies, we'll leave for Fort Smith and be there in three days."

"What do you have for supplies?" Murphy said as he built a fire.

"Flour, coffee, bacon, two rabbits I caught this morning, and several cans of beans," Belle said.

"Those rabbits won't keep," Murphy said. "I'll stew them up with some beans."

"I'll make a pot of coffee," Belle said.

An hour or so later, after tending to their horses, they sat down to eat in front of the fire.

"You make a decent stew, Murphy," Belle said.

"Tell me something, Belle. Where are all your people?" Murphy said.

"Off somewhere doing what they do," Belle said. "With that warrant hanging over my head, I can't chance being seen in public by the law."

"Blue Duck?" Murphy said.

"Ain't seen him," Belle said. "I heard he took a wife somewhere in Texas or thereabouts."

"This is your last chance, Belle," Murphy said. "Unless you want to hang in Judge Parker's court."

"I know it," Belle said. "I kind of have a hankering to move to Oklahoma for a spell and maybe settle down."

"Last chance, Belle," Murphy said. "If I have to come for you again, you go back in irons."

"You have my word," Belle said.

"Glad to hear it," Murphy said.

"Do you have anything to sweeten the coffee a bit?' Belle said.

Murphy removed a flask of whiskey from a saddlebag and splashed a bit into their coffee cups.

"Obliged," Belle said.

The spectacle of Murphy riding into Forth Smith with Belle Starr by his side had curious residents lining the streets.

Some cheered for Belle. Some booed Murphy. But everybody watched.

On the courthouse steps, a newspaper reporter attempted to take their photograph, but Murphy kicked the camera down the steps.

Murphy wasn't a fan of newspapers or reporters.

In the lobby of the courthouse, Murphy turned Belle over to Bass Reeves and Cal Whitson, two of Parker's most trusted US Marshals.

"Thank you for being a gentleman to me, Murphy," Belle said.

"Remember what I told you," Murphy said.

"I will," Belle said.

Murphy left the courthouse and walked to Boyle, mounted the saddle, ignored the crowd, and rode south to his farmhouse.

When he was within a hundred feet of the house, Murphy saw three people on the porch. Kai, his mother, and William Burke.

"I should shoot him on sight," Murphy said. "And I'm surprised that Kai didn't."

CHAPTER SIX

Kai brought a cup of coffee to Murphy as he sat in a chair beside Burke.

"I thought about shooting you," Murphy said.

"Makes two of us," Kai said.

"I didn't because I don't feel like sweating digging your grave," Murphy said.

"Makes two of us," Kai said.

"Why don't you tell me why you're here, Burke?" Murphy said.

From inside the house, the baby started to cry. "I'll see to her," Aideen said as she stood and entered the house.

"The governor of New York is running for president," Burke said.

"That fool," Murphy said. "I doubt he can tie his own shoes without being undone."

"Maybe so, but he's the front-runner according to the newspapers, and he's going on a six-week tour to pander for votes," Burke said. "New York, Philadelphia, Albany, Buffalo, Boston, and so on."

"That's a lot of babies to kiss," Murphy said. "And asses."

"Arthur is calling you back into service," Burke said.

"What for?" Murphy said.

"To take charge of Cleveland's security," Burke said.

"Cleveland's security?" Murphy said. "I don't give a f—"

"Murphy," Kai snapped.

27

Burke grinned as Murphy bit his tongue.

"Six weeks at top dollar," Burke said. "All you have to do is make sure he doesn't get shot."

"I'd dodge a bullet for him, not take one," Murphy said.

"When is enough, enough, Burke?" Kai said.

"Arthur leaves office in eight months," Burke said. "Your appointment expires when he steps down."

"Six weeks," Murphy said.

"Six and done," Burke said.

"How large a team?" Murphy said.

"Six men from the secret service handpicked by you," Burke said.

"Stay for dinner, Bill," Murphy said. "I'm going to take a bath."

"Cleveland wants to begin with Albany in three weeks," Burke said. "After that it's Manhattan, then Buffalo, and so on. You need to be in Albany a week early to pick your men and finalize the details."

Kai and Aideen had cleared the dinner table and were bringing out dessert and coffee. The baby was on Murphy's lap, and he handed her to Aideen.

"Thanks, Mother," Murphy said. "Burke, will you be in Albany?"

"I will," Burke said.

"Let's go a day or so early," Murphy said. "I'd like to stop and visit with Grant."

As she filled Murphy's coffee cup, Kai said, "That's a fine idea. It's too bad he can't meet your daughter."

Aideen, slicing chocolate cake, grinned at Kai.

"We don't know how much longer we'll have the general," Murphy said. "Kai, I know how much you hate New York, but maybe you can do this favor for me and come along with the baby and visit with Grant and Julia for a few days?"

"I do hate that place, but you are right. We don't know how much longer we will have General Grant," Kai said. "Aideen, will you come and help me with the baby?"

"That's a fine idea," Murphy said. "Burke, let's take our coffee and cake to the porch."

After Murphy and Burke left the table, Aideen and Kai looked at each other and laughed.

"They only think they are in charge," Aideen said.

Murphy read the complete schedule Burke produced from his briefcase. Thirty cities in six weeks meant a lot of time spent on a train and in hotels. The six men assigned to the detail needed to be experienced men who knew how to follow orders and how to handle the unexpected emergency.

"Tell Arthur I need the six best men he has," Murphy said. "No first-year men and no married men. I don't want some man worried about his wife and baby."

"I'll tell him," Burke said. "I'd best get back to town before it gets dark."

"I'll see you in Albany in two weeks," Murphy said.

Murphy sat on the bed and watched Kai brush her hair at her dressing table. He was always fascinated how, when she let her hair down, it reached the middle of her back.

"I appreciate you coming along to visit Grant," Murphy said. "I heard he won't last but maybe three or four more months."

"We owe it to him to see him and to comfort Julia," Kai said.

Finished with her hair, she set the brush aside and stood up from the chair. She turned, looked at Murphy, and removed her robe.

"Maybe you can repay the favor by pleasing me," Kai said.

CHAPTER SEVEN

Murphy, Kai, Aideen, and the baby met Burke at the railroad station in Manhattan on the West Side of the island.

Aideen had gone home to Tennessee for two days to check on Michael, and also to pack the appropriate clothing for the trip.

Burke rented a large coach for the trip to Wilton, New York, where Grant lived in the home Grant called Mount McGregor. The ride took about two hours.

The Mount McGregor home was quiet when they arrived. Julia met them at the front gate near the stables. She was close to tears as she hugged Murphy and Kai.

"He is in his study, writing his memoirs," Julia said. "But his voice is very weak, and you have to stand close to hear him."

Julia took them to the study. Grant immediately perked up at the sight of Murphy. He was thin and a shell of his former self, but Grant stood to shake hands and hugged Kai and Aideen.

"This is our daughter, Aideen, named for Murphy's mother," Kai said.

"A fine baby girl," Grant said, barely above a whisper.

"Kai, maybe you and Aideen can help me prepare lunch?" Julia said.

After the women left the study, Grant sat behind his desk. "I can't have any but I would appreciate it if you men had a drink on my behalf," he said.

Murphy went to the bar, poured an ounce of bourbon into two glasses, and handed one to Burke.

"To you, General," Murphy said.

After sipping their drinks, Murphy and Burke took chairs.

"How are the memoirs going, General?" Burke said.

"I need months to finish," Grant said. "And I'm afraid I may not live long enough to complete them."

"You will, General," Murphy said.

"I have to," Grant said. "If I am to leave Julia provided for after I am gone."

"She will be, General," Murphy said. "I will make sure she gets every penny coming to her."

Grant nodded. "I know you will," he said. "And I have done as you asked and left you out of the memoirs."

"That's appreciated," Murphy said.

"I'm afraid I won't be able to eat much, but let's go see what the women prepared for lunch," Grant said.

After lunch, Grant went for a nap and Julia, Kai, and Aideen saw Murphy and Burke to the coach.

"We will see you in Albany in three days," Kai said.

The mood in the coach on the ride back to Manhattan was gloomy. Both Murphy and Burke knew Grant wouldn't survive the year. To see a once-great general and president waste away to nothing was gut wrenching.

The coach let them off in front of the railroad station. The driver removed their luggage from the large trunk, and Burke offered the driver a handsome tip.

"Our train will get us to Albany by ten tonight," Burke said. "We can have supper on board."

After boarding the train and checking their luggage, Murphy and Burke killed time in the gentlemen's car with a game of chess. The game ended in a draw. At eight o'clock, they went to the dining car for supper.

The waiter recommended the baked chicken.

"Tell me something, Murphy. Not counting the war, how many men have you killed?" Burke said.

"Is it important?" Murphy said.

"It is to me," Burke said.

"Why?"

"I suppose I'd like to know how many men you killed on my orders," Burke said.

"Again, why?" Murphy said.

"I suppose I'd like to know that the men you've killed in the line of duty somehow made the country better, safer," Burke said. "So that I can retire with a clear conscience."

"I never killed anybody in the line of duty who didn't try to kill me," Murphy said. "Your conscience is clear."

"Did you bring a bottle of that fine whiskey your father makes?" Burke said.

"Two."

"May I suggest we retire to the gentlemen's car for a drink after dinner," Burke said.

Grant ate very little at dinner and retired to his study to work on his memoirs.

Kai, Aideen, and Julia took coffee on the porch.

"Hiram is bound and determined to finish his memoirs before he dies," Julia said. "But I am afraid the strain of writing them will take him sooner than expected."

"He shares the same stubborn streak as Murphy," Kai said. "Once his mind is made up, he is unmovable."

"Men like Hiram and Murphy are becoming a rare breed," Julia said. "When he was needed most to lead Lincoln's army, Hiram answered the call. Afterward, when the country needed a man to reunite the country, he again answered the call. Murphy fought for him in the war and protected him afterward. Men like those two are vanishing quickly, I'm afraid."

From inside the house, the baby suddenly cried.

Kai stood, but Julia said, "Allow me. Please. It's been a long time since I tended a baby."

Kai nodded and Julia entered the house.

"She is right about one thing," Aideen said. "Men like General Grant and my son are becoming a rare breed."

Murphy and Burke checked into the Stanwix Hotel, the oldest hotel in Albany.

"We'll meet with Cleveland after breakfast," Burke said.

"I can hardly contain my excitement," Murphy said.

"A nightcap?" Burke said.

"Why not?" Murphy said.

After dropping off their luggage, Burke went to Murphy's room, where Murphy poured two glasses of his father's bourbon.

"I'm to make three stops with you to measure Cleveland's popularity and then report to Arthur," Burke said.

"Are you serious about retiring?" Murphy said.

"I am," Burke said. "I'm tired of the game. I have some years left in me; I'd like to enjoy them without the worry of Washington politics. I thought I'd go home, buy a little house, and just do nothing."

"Wouldn't that be nice," Murphy said. "To just do nothing."

Burke raised his glass. "To doing nothing," he said. "May it be everything I've dreamed of."

CHAPTER EIGHT

Murphy and Burke met Grover Cleveland in his office at the New York State Capitol on State Street in Albany.

Cleveland spent considerable time outlining his plans to fundraise and give speeches from Albany to Ohio during the six-week tour.

"After a break in late summer, I will resume the tour out west as far as California and north to Seattle," Cleveland said.

Murphy looked at Burke and then at Cleveland. "I agreed only to this six weeks," he said.

"I'm sure during the six weeks, Murphy will be able to train a suitable replacement," Burke said. "A dozen men from Arthur will be reporting tomorrow from whom Murphy will select six. I'm sure one of them can be elevated to take charge."

Cleveland looked at Murphy. "I am aware of the impact you had on the New York City Police Department not long ago when you apprehended that serial murderer," he said. "That's why I wanted you. However, if you can train a suitable replacement, I see no reason why you can't return home."

Burke noticed the purple vein expose itself on the side of Murphy's neck and sighed. "Governor, we'll take our leave now, as there is much to prepare," he said.

"Stupid, pompous ass," Murphy said as he and Burke walked down the capitol steps.

"Cleveland is a politician," Burke said.

"God save us from them all, as they will undo the future as sure as our ancestors did the past," Murphy said.

"Come on, we have much to cover," Burke said.

They climbed aboard the waiting buggy, and the driver took them to their hotel. They ordered lunch from room service and took it in Burke's room.

Burke had a briefcase full of maps. They studied the street map of Albany. "The route from the capitol building to the banquet hall where Cleveland will be speaking is only six blocks," he said.

Murphy looked at the map. "Those six blocks are all main streets with heavy traffic," he said. "Anybody with a rifle and a window could take out Cleveland in his carriage. We'll take the back streets."

Murphy traced a route with a pencil to the banquet hall.

"And a different route afterward to his home," Murphy said.

Burke peered at the map.

"I want four men inside the coach with Cleveland," Murphy said. "I will ride with the driver. The route will remain secret until it's time to leave."

After lunch, Murphy said, "I'd like to see Cleveland's coach."

The governor had a regular buggy, an open coach and a large, closed coach with glass windows for winter travel.

The stable manager for the governor showed Murphy and Burke the closed coach.

"I want heavy curtains hung on both windows," Murphy said. "Cleveland sits in the middle where a lucky shot won't hit him."

"It will be dark in there at night with the windows covered," the stable manager said.

"Is Cleveland afraid of the dark?" Murphy said. "We can bring two lanterns and set them on the floor. Just make sure those curtains are black and heavy."

On the way back to the hotel, Murphy said, "Burke, can you send telegrams to all locations where Cleveland will be speaking and make sure they have an enclosed coach with glass windows?"

"And you wonder why you keep getting called back," Burke said.

Late in the afternoon, Murphy smoked his pipe while he sat at the desk in his hotel room and cleaned his Colt revolver. It was custom made for him to his own specifications. Those specifications jumped the price from thirty-five dollars to a staggering one hundred and twenty-five.

Besides a hair trigger, the grip was made to fit his very large hand like a glove. The wheel action was like a finely tuned machine, and he had designed the sights himself. Even the holster was custom made, and it fit the Colt so the draw was without snag.

The Colt was his favorite among all the firearms he owned. As he was reassembling it, Burke knocked on his hotel room door.

"Enter," Murphy said.

Burke walked in and said, "I've sent thirty plus telegrams concerning the coach for the governor," he said.

"Do you have a list of the men coming tomorrow?" Murphy said.

"I do."

"Bring it when we go to dinner," Murphy said.

Burke looked at the Colt on the desk. "Still use that same Colt," he said.

"Find me a better one, and I'll switch," Murphy said.

"I'll meet you at seven in the hotel restaurant," Burke said.

Murphy read the list of names submitted by Arthur for Cleveland's security detail. Every man was between twenty-five and thirty-one years old.

"Some of these men are young enough to be my sons," Murphy said.

"And how old were you when Grant appointed you to head his security detail fifteen years ago?" Burke said.

"And which war did these men spend three years in, shedding blood?" Murphy said.

Finished with dinner, Burke said, "Let's have a drink on the porch and enjoy the cooler night air."

Murphy and Burke took drinks of bourbon to the porch of the hotel where Burke lit a cigar and Murphy his pipe.

"Where are we staging the men tomorrow?" Murphy said.

"I reserved a meeting room here at the hotel," Burke said.

"What time is their train due?"

"Ten o'clock," Burke said. "We'll meet them with two coaches."

"Let them walk," Murphy said.

"Walk? Why?" Burke said.

"If they can't find their way to the hotel on their own, we don't need them," Murphy said.

CHAPTER NINE

Murphy and Burke waited in the meeting room at the hotel. They enjoyed a nice breakfast and then took coffee at a table in the room.

Burke smoked a cigar, Murphy his pipe.

"More coffee?" Burke said.

"Please," Murphy said.

Burke got the pot and filled both cups.

"It's ten-thirty and it's a five minute walk from the railroad to the hotel," Murphy said.

"Give them five minutes and I'll . . ." Burke said just as the door opened and the dozen agents filed in.

"Is this the . . . is one of you men Mr. Burke?" one of them said.

"I'm Burke."

"We were told we'd be met by coach," the agent said.

"And how long did you hoopleheads stand there sucking your thumbs before you realized coaches weren't coming?" Murphy said.

"I don't care for your remark," the man said.

Murphy walked to the man. The man stood a half-foot shorter than Murphy. "Is that so?" Murphy said.

The man looked up at Murphy. "And you are, sir?" he said.

"Murphy. I head this detail," Murphy said. "And if you don't like my tone, I suggest you take some measure to change it to your liking."

Burke sighed.

"I didn't come here to argue," the man said.

"That is exactly right," Murphy said. "You came here to take a bullet for the governor of New York should the need arise, the same as you would for President Arthur. Any questions?"

There were no questions.

"Good. Let's get started. Grab some coffee and come to the table," Murphy said.

Once everybody was settled at the table, Murphy covered the map and route to the banquet.

"After lunch we will walk the route to familiarize ourselves with the streets and buildings," Murphy said.

An agent held up his hand.

"Yes," Murphy said.

"We were told that only six of us will be selected for this detail," he said. "How will you determine which six?"

"Good question," Murphy said. "The answer is all twelve of you will be selected for this detail."

Burke sat up in his chair. "How?" he said.

"One team works the detail while the second team goes to the next city to scout the location and streets," Murphy said. "Like scouts in the army surveying a possible future battle site. We can even rotate the teams to keep the men sharp."

"That makes sense," Burke said. "Arthur will have to be convinced to pay the extra tab."

"Not if Cleveland is paying for it," Murphy said. "Okay, you men, I'm sure you want to check into your rooms and get settled. We'll meet in the restaurant in the lobby at one o'clock. After lunch, we'll walk the route."

Murphy led the way from the governor's mansion to the banquet hall.

"The reason we are taking a longer route is because the side

39

streets are less crowded, and anyone out to do harm to Cleveland will be easier to spot," Murphy said. "Make note of the rooftops, alleyways, and windows where a possible sniper might take position."

The men, including Burke, looked up at rooftops and windows and at alleyways.

"Each man pick where you think it's easiest for a sniper to fire on Cleveland," Murphy said.

When they reached the banquet hall, Murphy gathered the men in the small park across the street.

"Let's discuss the locations where you think a sniper might hide," Murphy said.

Three men picked the same rooftop. Two men picked the same alleyway. The rest picked different rooftops and alleyways.

"All good choices," Murphy said. "Let me pose a question to you. Would it be feasible to imagine a plot to murder the future president might require more than one shooter?"

All twelve agents agreed.

"And they might have one or two snipers along the route, only to discover at the last minute the route has been changed," Murphy said. "Where might a third sniper be waiting?"

The twelve agents and Burke were stumped.

"Even if they knew the route and had two snipers on rooftops, they will quickly realize they don't have a shot through the covered glass windows of the coach, and it's up to the third man," Murphy said. "Cleveland will be most vulnerable when he exits the coach. The man on the roof of the banquet hall has a clear line of sight."

Everybody looked at the roof of the three-story banquet hall across the street.

"Wouldn't it make sense to have one of us on the banquet hall roof?" an agent said.

"And I am very glad you volunteered for the job," Murphy said.

The men laughed.

"So now when the advance team travels to the next stop, you know what to look for," Murphy said. "That's all for today."

After dinner, a telegram arrived for Murphy. He read it on the porch as he and Burke took coffee.

"Kai and my mother will be here tomorrow for a quick visit," Murphy said.

"With news of Grant, I hope," Burke said.

Murphy reached into his jacket pocket for the flask of bourbon he tucked away and splashed some into their coffee cups.

"To the general," Murphy said.

"To the general," Burke said and lifted his cup.

CHAPTER TEN

Murphy, Kai, Aiden, Burke, and the baby took dinner in the hotel restaurant, although the baby slept in her carrier beside Kai.

"The general is so weak," Kai said. "Sometimes his voice is barely a whisper."

"Will he finish his memoirs?" Burke said.

"I believe he won't allow himself to die until they are completed," Kai said.

"What will you do when I'm away?" Murphy said to Kai.

"I thought I would spend some time with Aideen and Michael," Kai said. "I can send one of your men from the farm to stay at the house in Fort Smith while I'm away. He can tend to the horses and keep an eye on things."

"That's a good idea," Murphy said.

"We thought we'd stay over and attend this banquet and see what Cleveland has to say," Aideen said.

"Burke, can you get them tickets?" Murphy said.

"They can sit at my table with Cleveland's people," Burke said. "But what of the baby?"

"The hotel provides a nanny when needed," Kai said.

"Then I will escort you ladies to the event while Murphy tends to his business of security," Burke said.

Murphy watched Kai brush her hair at the dressing table in the hotel room. The baby slept in her traveling basket beside the bed on the floor.

"Ask my father to send my foreman to stay at our house," Murphy said. "He's the only one Boyle will allow to feed and brush him without getting violent and nasty."

Kai smiled at Murphy. "Horse and owner are a lot alike," he said.

"Come to bed," Murphy said as he removed his pants.

Kai stood and removed her robe. She stood on her toes to kiss Murphy and he lowered her to the bed.

At that moment, the baby awoke and started to cry for food.

"Horse, owner, and baby are all a lot alike, I should have said," Kai said as she stood up.

"Where is my son?" Aideen said.

She and Kai were seated at Burke's table.

"You won't see him," Kai said. "He's there, but you'll never see him unless he wants to be seen."

"I guess there are many things my son has done in his life I am unaware of," Aideen said.

"It's best that way," Kai said.

After dinner, Cleveland came on stage and made his sixty-minute-long speech.

While Burke took Kai and Aideen back to the hotel, Murphy led the team taking Cleveland to his residence.

Cleveland invited Murphy into his residence for a quick meeting in the study. Cleveland poured two small glasses of brandy, which Murphy disliked but accepted.

"The country has changed a great deal since the war ended," Cleveland said. "Much of the west is now civilized, and the south is once again intact and productive."

Murphy took a small sip of the brandy. It went down like cough syrup.

"Soon many territories will be admitted to the union, and our country will continue to grow," Cleveland said. "I studied your record after Arthur recommended you to me. You're a dying breed, Murphy. The day of your kind is quickly coming to an end. Civilization is taking over where your kind once ruled."

"My kind?" Murphy said.

"No offense intended, Murphy," Cleveland said. "But I am talking about the days of the gunfighter. They are over and have no place in society anymore."

"When did they ever?" Murphy said.

"My point is that if you intend to stay in the secret service when I'm elected, we must reach an understanding," Cleveland said. "Professionalism first and the gun second."

"That's a discussion for after you win the election," Murphy said. "For now my focus is seeing that you stay alive."

"Quite right," Cleveland said. "Good night, Murphy."

"Pompous ass," Murphy said. "Next time he goes out the window headfirst."

"He's a politician, Murphy," Burke said. "He fears that if he isn't talking, you might forget about him."

"The west is civilized?" Murphy said. "Has he ever set foot in the west?"

They were having a glass of bourbon on the porch of the hotel. Kai and Aideen were in their rooms.

"Go up to your wife," Burke said. "She is leaving in the morning, and I'm sure you'd rather be with her than me."

"I make it a point never to go to her when I'm mad," Murphy said.

"Then you might as well live in separate houses," Burke said.

"I do believe I will take your advice," Murphy said and stood up.

CHAPTER ELEVEN

"Aideen will stay with me until your foreman arrives in Fort Smith," Kai said.

"Look after Mother and the baby," Murphy said.

After Murphy kissed Kai and Aideen and the baby, Kai looked at Burke. "The next time you come calling, hat in hand, I will use that shotgun," she said.

"I will remember that," Burke said.

Kai, Aideen, and the baby boarded the train.

"Well," Burke said to Murphy. "Let's go to work."

"Your private train leaves at eight tomorrow morning," Burke said. "It arrives in Buffalo at one in the afternoon. That leaves plenty of time to rest and prepare for the speaking banquet at seven p.m."

"The second team has already left for Buffalo to scout out the route and ready the hotel," Murphy said. "The first team, myself, and Mr. Burke will ride on your train, along with your staff."

Cleveland nodded. "Very efficient," he said. "And now I have appointments."

"We'll be by at seven to take you to the train," Murphy said.

As they walked down the capitol building steps, Burke said, "What shall we do with the rest of the day?"

"I'm taking the men shooting," Murphy said.

★ ★ ★ ★ ★

The Albany Police Department had a fine shooting range. Murphy made arrangements to take his six-man crew shooting in the afternoon.

Murphy had each man fire a box of fifty rounds at targets set seven, fourteen, and twenty-one feet away.

Each of the six men had a Colt Peacemaker. Every man proved capable of hitting the center of the target from the three distances.

The men shot the way they were trained by the secret service instructors.

"A question for you men," Murphy said. "Say the man attempting to shoot the president was thirty or more feet away, would you be able to stop him?"

"Thirty or more feet with a Colt?" an agent said.

"No time to take careful aim. How would you handle it?" Murphy said. "One of you men, move the target to thirty-five feet."

An agent moved the target to thirty-five feet. Murphy stood facing the six agents.

"You're at the door or on stage in the wings," Murphy said. "You spot a man with a gun. He cocks and aims at the president. What do you do?"

Murphy drew his Colt, spun, cocked, and then fired six shots into the center of the target thirty-five feet away.

"You put the man down, is what you do," Murphy said.

The men looked at him.

"We know I can do it," Murphy said. "Show me you can do it."

Murphy was in his room, packing his gear and clothes for the trip to Buffalo on the morrow.

Once packed, he sat at the desk with a glass of whiskey,

smoked his pipe, and cleaned his Colt revolver and Winchester rifle.

There was a knock on the door. "Yes," Murphy said.

"A telegram for you just arrived," a male voice said.

Murphy went to the door, gave the man a dollar, and took the telegram. He returned to the desk, sat, and opened the envelope. It was from Kai. She, Aideen, and the baby arrived safely in Fort Smith. His foreman would be there in two days, and then they would travel to Tennessee.

Murphy removed a bottle of bourbon from his suitcase, left his room, walked down the hall to Burke's room, and knocked on the door.

"Yes," Burke said.

"It's Murphy," Murphy said.

"Come in," Burke said.

Murphy opened the door and entered the room. "I thought a nightcap was in order," Murphy said.

"You thought correctly," Burke said.

Murphy walked to the dresser where two glasses rested beside the water basin. He added two ounces of bourbon to both glasses and handed one to Burke.

"How far are you coming with us?" Murphy said.

"Buffalo to Manhattan and then to Philadelphia," Burke said. "Then I'll report to Arthur on Cleveland's popularity."

"Were you serious about retiring after the election?" Murphy said.

"Yes," Burke said. "I'm thinking of Florida."

"Florida? What is in Florida?" Murphy said.

"Sunshine," Burke said. "Twelve months of the year. My old bones can't take winter like they did twenty years ago."

Murphy and Burke sipped from their glasses.

"By the time young Aideen is eighteen, you'll understand what I mean," Burke said. "So take my advice, Murphy. When

Arthur is out, your time is up. Do not reenlist under any circumstances. You've done your time. You owe nobody."

Murphy lifted the bottle of bourbon. "Another shot?" he said.

"Indeed," Burke said.

CHAPTER TWELVE

Three more stops, and the tour would be over. The men had learned well, and Murphy felt confident they could handle the second tour without his help.

What he realized being away from home on such a mundane task was how much he missed Kai and the baby.

Burke was right. He'd done his time. It was time for the next generation to take the reins. It was time for him to step aside and be with his family.

Michael Murphy took fierce pride in the bourbon he distilled. He chose his land for the freshwater stream that ran down from the mountains. The better the water, the better the bourbon, was his philosophy.

He grew his own corn on a thousand acres of land and purchased another thousand acres from his son. Still, that wasn't enough.

He employed four distillers, a dozen farmers, and six men who tended to the warehouse.

The warehouse presently held four hundred barrels of bourbon. One hundred were ready to transport to the bottler. He hired a freight company in town to take the barrels to the railroad.

Michael went to the warehouse to speak to the men and select the barrels.

John Moats and Tom Holland, two men who hired on a few

months back, were rotating barrels from the first tier to the second.

"Afternoon, men," Michael said. "The freight company will be here tomorrow morning some time. We need to get one hundred barrels ready for them. The oldest one hundred will do."

"We'll need more men," Holland said.

"Four more are on the way," Michael said. "Let's get started."

The work was hard. Barrels had to be rolled outside and arranged in stacks of two. It took six men, plus Michael, until dark to move the one hundred barrels to the staging area.

"You men earned a bonus in your pay this month," Michael told the six men.

Aideen and Kai held dinner until Michael returned. "I have a hot bath ready for you," Aideen said. "We'll hold dinner until you're ready."

"Thank you, dear," Michael said.

Michael limped up the stairs to the bathtub room.

"He still thinks he's thirty," Aideen said.

"Now I know where Murphy gets it from," Kai said.

"Menfolk think they will stay young forever," Aideen said. "And they do up here," she said and tapped her head. "Let's set the table."

Holland and Moats sat on a bench in front of the bunkhouse and drank from a bottle of whiskey.

"How much longer are we going to bust our backs for this rich asshole?" Moats said.

"Keep your voice down," Holland said. "The men inside have big ears."

"Screw them, too," Moats said.

"He'll ride into town tomorrow to the bank," Holland said. "He'll collect for those hundred barrels from the bottling company. He'll be fat and happy after that. Tomorrow night we'll do the job."

"Then we go to California as we planned," Moats said.

"And do some living along the way," Holland said.

"I'm all for doing some living," Moats said as he drank some whiskey.

"That was a fine supper, ladies," Michael said.

"Would you like coffee, Michael?" Kai said.

"I would," Michael said.

"Take coffee on the porch while I tend to the dishes," Kai said.

"It's a fine night. May I take the baby?" Aideen said.

"Please," Kai said. "I'll bring out the coffee."

Michael and Aideen, with the baby in her carry crib, went to the porch. Michael and Aideen took chairs.

"Our son married well," Michael said.

"That he did," Aideen said.

"Of course he needs an heir, a son," Michael said.

"Girls can be heirs, too, Michael," Aideen said.

"Boys carry on the name," Michael said.

"Your brother in Ohio has six sons," Aideen said. "The name is in no present danger."

Kai opened the screen door holding a tray with a pot and two cups.

"Thank you, dear," Aideen said.

"When is my son coming home?" Michael said.

"Within a week," Kai said. "He wants to stop in Fort Smith first for his horse."

"It will be good to have him back," Michael said.

Kai smiled. "It sure will," she said.

CHAPTER THIRTEEN

The freight company required six large wagons with teams of four mules per wagon. Loading the wagons took several hours. When the work was done, Michael saddled his horse and rode along with the wagons to town.

He told Aideen and Kai he would be back around four in the afternoon. Before leaving, he told the warehouse crew they could have the rest of the day off.

Holland and Moats waited for the other four men and the foreman to ride to town before they packed up their gear. The put on their holsters and walked from the bunkhouse to the house.

They didn't knock on the door, but simply opened it and walked in.

Aideen and Kai were in the kitchen, baking bread. Aideen noticed them first. "What do you men want?" she said.

"Cooperation," Holland said.

"Who else is in the house?" Moats said.

"My baby daughter," Kai said.

"We're all going to the living room where it's nice and comfortable," Holland said.

"You men leave this house right now," Aideen said.

Moats pulled his gun and cocked it. "Move," he said.

Aideen and Kai went to the living room, followed by Moats and Holland.

"Got any food?" Moats said.

"Of course we have food," Aideen said.

"You, Grandma, fix us some grub," Holland said.

"Best go with her," Moats said. "I'll watch this one."

Aideen and Holland went to the kitchen. Moats looked at Kai.

"You half Indian?" Moats said.

"A quarter Navajo," Kai said.

"Where's that baby you said you had?" Moats said.

"In her crib in the bedroom," Kai said.

"Let's go get her," Moats said.

Kai, followed by Moats, went to her bedroom on the second floor where the baby slept in her crib.

"All right, bring her down," Moats said.

Kai lifted the baby, and they returned to the living room.

"No, the kitchen," Moats said.

They went to the kitchen. "How are you coming with the grub?" Moats said.

"A few minutes," Aideen said.

"Pour us some coffee," Holland said.

Aideen filled two cups and set them on the table. Holland looked at Kai. "You, sit," he said. "And keep that baby quiet."

Kai took a chair.

"If you're after money, we keep very little in the house," Aideen said.

"Grandma, if I don't ask you a question, you don't talk," Holland said.

Aideen looked at Holland. "Are you ready to eat?" she said.

"Dish it up," Holland said.

Aideen served each man four fried eggs, bacon, potatoes, and coffee.

"Now you sit right there next to the squaw and be quiet," Moats said.

Holland and Moats ate quickly. Aideen cleared the table.

"What time will he be back?" Holland said.

"Around four," Aideen said.

"You women, all you have to do is be quiet and do what we say, and no one gets hurt," Holland said.

The baby woke up and started to cry. "She needs milk," Kai said.

"Give it to her," Moats said. "Just shut her up."

Aideen took a bottle from the icebox and warmed it on the stove. Then she handed it to Kai.

"You rich people make me sick, with your fancy iceboxes and big houses," Holland said.

"We worked hard for everything we have," Aideen said.

"Your husband keep money in the house?" Moats said.

"I told you. Very little," Aideen said.

"If we look and find money, I'll beat you," Moats said.

"Go ahead and look," Aideen said.

"We'll wait," Holland said. "In the living room where we'll all get cozy."

Aideen and Kai sat on the sofa. Kai kept the baby on her lap. Moats sat in a chair and watched Aideen and Kai. Holland kept watch at the window.

"You sure he said four o'clock?" Holland said.

"I'm sure," Aideen said. "When my husband sets a time, you can bet he'll keep it, for all the good it will do you."

Holland turned and looked at Aideen. "Explain that remark," he said.

"Do you think my husband is going to bring all that money to the house?" Aideen said. "He'll deposit it in the bank and bring home a hundred dollars at most."

"You let us worry about that," Holland said. "Now shut up and bring us some whiskey."

Aideen went to the bar and filled two glasses with bourbon. She gave one to Moats, the other to Holland.

Moats continued to stare at Kai. Finally he stood, walked to the window, and stood beside Holland. "That squaw is a fine looking woman," Moats said.

"What of it?" Holland said.

"I think I'd like to take her to the bedroom for a lay," Moats said.

"It's twenty of three by that wall clock," Holland said. "No time for such."

"After then," Moats said.

"Keep your wits, and go watch them women," Holland said. "No, wait. I see a rider coming."

"He's early," Moats said.

"All right, get ready," Holland said. "And keep them women quiet."

Moats walked to the sofa and drew his gun. "One word, I shoot both of you, so best be quiet."

Holland kept watch at the window. He waited until Michael had dismounted and tied his horse to the hitching post before he went to the door and stood aside.

The door opened and Michael walked in. He looked at Aideen and Kai on the sofa and Moats holding a gun on them.

"Moats, what is this?" Michael said.

Behind Michael, Holland stuck his gun in Michael's back. "What do you think it is?" Holland said. "Move over there with your wife and the squaw."

Michael walked to the sofa. "What do you men want?" he said.

"What do you think we want?" Holland said. "We want money."

"I don't keep much in the house," Michael said. "A few hundred dollars at most."

"Don't play stupid, old man," Holland said. "We know you sold all that whiskey today. How much did you make?"

"Twenty-two thousand dollars," Michael said.

Holland grinned. "Hear that, Moats? He's a rich man."

"That money isn't here," Michael said. "It's in the bank."

"Looks like you're going to have to make a withdrawal," Holland said.

"The bank closes at three," Michael said.

"We know that," Holland said. "We also know it opens at nine. At nine tomorrow morning, you will withdraw twenty-two thousand and bring it to us pronto. Make no mistake. If we see the law or anybody else but you, we shoot these women. Am I understood?"

"Yes," Michael said.

"Now we'll all spend the night cozy-like here in the living room," Holland said. "Do as we say and nobody gets hurt. But if you think for one damn second I won't shoot you all, think twice."

"You'll have your money," Michael said.

"Good. Now have a seat," Holland said.

CHAPTER FOURTEEN

After an uncomfortable night of sleeping on the sofa and chairs, Aideen and Kai made breakfast and served it in the living room.

"I have a request," Michael said.

"What is it?" Holland said.

"I would like to shave and change my shirt," Michael said. "It would seem odd to the bank if I went in otherwise."

"Moats, go with him," Holland said.

Twenty minutes later, Michael stood before Aideen and Kai. "Don't worry," he said. "I'll be back with the money, and they will leave. You'll be all right."

At the door, Holland said, "Remember what I told you about the law. No matter if we get killed, we'll kill the women first. And that's what you remember."

"I remember," Michael said.

Murphy stretched out in the bed in his sleeping car. The final speaking engagement ended yesterday, and he was headed to Albany before taking the train to Tennessee.

The six weeks had passed without incident. Murphy was no judge of politicians, but it appeared to him that Cleveland had a good chance of winning the White House.

Before boarding the train, Murphy sent a telegram to Kai telling her he was on the way home and would be there in three days' time.

★　★　★　★　★

Close to one o'clock in the afternoon, Michael returned with the money. He dismounted, tied his horse to the post, and entered the house when Holland opened the door.

"You got the money?" Holland said.

"I have it," Michael said.

"Give it to me," Holland said.

Michael withdrew the fat leather wallet from his jacket pocket and handed it to Holland.

"Over to the sofa," Holland said.

Michael sat between Aideen and Kai. Aideen held the baby.

"We're going to tie you up," Holland said. "You'll be found soon enough by your hands when they come for something."

"Wait a minute, Tom," Moats said. He grabbed Kai by the arm and yanked her to her feet. "I want a turn with this squaw first."

Michael jumped up and punched Moats, knocking him to the floor.

"Animal," Michael said.

Moats drew his gun and shot Michael in the chest. Michael fell backward to the sofa.

"Michael! My God, no!" Aideen said.

"Now you done it," Holland said. "Let's get out of here."

Holland and Moats ran to the door. Kai followed. From the steps, she shouted, "My husband will find you, the both of you. When he does, he will kill you both. They call him the Regulator. Do you know what that is? A killer of men. You remember that and take it to your graves, you fucking bastards."

Aideen came up behind Kai. "Saddle a horse and ride to town for the doctor," she said. "Hurry."

Aideen and Kai assisted the doctor after bringing Michael to the bedroom on the first floor.

"He's lost a lot of blood," the doctor said.

"What about the bullet?" Aideen said.

"It's lodged up against his heart," the doctor said.

"But you will operate?" Aideen said.

"If I try to remove that bullet, it will kill him," the doctor said.

"And if you don't?" Aideen said.

"He'll die in his own due course," the doctor said.

Aideen looked at Kai. Then she turned back to the doctor. "That's no choice, Doctor," Aideen said. "My husband has been a fighter all his life, and he would not want to go out like a beaten dog. Operate. Give him a fighting chance. Please."

The doctor nodded. "Who will assist me?" he said.

"Both of us," Kai said.

Around one in the morning, Murphy gave up trying to sleep. He dressed and took his pipe to the gentlemen's car. There were just three men in the car. They were playing cards and having a drink.

Murphy ordered a bourbon from the bar and took a chair by a window. He had a feeling of dread that he couldn't shake or identify. The last time he'd had such a feeling was during the war before a battle. The feeling would drape over him like a blanket and wouldn't leave until the battle started.

The war had ended nearly twenty years ago and so did the feeling of dread. Until tonight, and that didn't make sense. All he was doing was riding home on a train.

Why the heavy feeling of disaster hanging over his head?

The game at the table broke up and Murphy was alone in the car. He ordered another drink and stayed there until morning.

Chapter Fifteen

Exhausted, the doctor fell asleep in a chair next to the bed. Michael had survived the surgery, but he was weak, very weak.

The doctor woke when the morning sun hit him in the face. The first thing he did was to check on Michael.

The man was still alive, but barely. How his body drew breath was a mystery because he had no godly right being alive.

The doctor left the bedroom. The house was quiet, cold. Aideen was asleep on the sofa. Kai was making coffee in the kitchen.

"Is he . . . ?" Kai said.

"He's alive, but for how much longer only God knows," the doctor said.

"Sit down. I'll pour you some coffee and then wake Aideen," Kai said.

"I'm awake," Aideen said as she entered the kitchen. "I heard what you said, Doctor. Can I sit with him?"

The doctor nodded. "I'll be in directly," he said.

Aideen left the kitchen. Kai filled two cups with coffee, and she and the doctor took chairs.

"Is there nothing to be done?" Kai said.

"Pray," the doctor said.

Murphy had sent a telegram to his foreman staying at the Fort Smith home to meet him at the train station with a buggy.

When Murphy stepped off the train, the foreman was at the

end of the platform. Murphy carried his two large suitcases to the buggy.

"How are you, Mr. Murphy?" the foreman said.

"Tired, Sam. It was a long six weeks," Murphy said.

They loaded Murphy's bags into the buggy, climbed aboard, and Sam took the reins.

The drive to the house took about an hour.

"Sam, can you stay on here for another week?" Murphy said. "I'll be back with Kai by then."

"No problem, Mr. Murphy," Sam said.

"Boyle give you any trouble?" Murphy said.

"He'll let me feed him, but he won't let me brush him or put a saddle on him," Sam said. "At best, he'll let me walk him to the corral."

"He'll need a good run," Murphy said.

When they reached the house, Boyle was in the corral. At the sight of Murphy, Boyle perked up and ran around the corral as if to show Murphy how excited he was.

Murphy opened the gate and Boyle ran to him. "Hey, boy," Murphy said as Boyle nuzzled him.

"Let me change out of this suit and we'll go for a ride," Murphy said.

Aideen held Michael's hand as Kai and the doctor stood by and watched. Michael's breathing was so shallow, his chest barely moved.

With a final breath, Michael's chest went still.

Aideen lowered her head to Michael's chest and cried.

With tears running down her face, Kai looked away.

"He's with God now," the doctor said. "May God keep his soul."

Murphy ran Boyle for about five miles, following the stream

flowing beside the house. Then he dismounted, removed the saddle, and gave Boyle a thorough brushing.

"Tomorrow we go to Tennessee for a few days," Murphy said. "School will be starting soon on the reservation, and we need to bring Kai back so she can teach the children."

After brushing Boyle, Murphy sat under a tree and lit his pipe. Boyle ate some grass and then went to the stream for a drink.

"You know, Boyle, when I retire you retire," Murphy said.

Boyle turned his head to look at Murphy.

"Your job will be to see after the girls and sire some foals," Murphy said.

Boyle whinnied.

"You're right. Let's go," Murphy said.

Murphy mounted the saddle and tugged on the reins.

Sam showed Murphy the letters and telegrams from the men he left in charge while he was in Fort Smith.

"The harvest should be enough for two hundred barrels. Two foals were born only last week," Sam said.

"You've done a good job for me, Sam," Murphy said. "I am grateful. After the harvest, I will see that you and all the men get a handsome bonus."

"Thank you, Mr. Murphy," Sam said.

"I believe I will have a bath and then maybe some supper," Murphy said. "What have we in the house?"

"While I was waiting for the train, I picked up some thick steaks," Sam said.

"Excellent," Murphy said.

"She'll sleep now," the doctor said. "I'm leaving you this bottle of sleeping powder. When she wakes up, see that she stays calm. If need be, give her a dose. The instructions are on the bottle."

"Thank you, Doctor," Kai said. "Please tell the sheriff what has happened."

"I will. About the body?" the doctor said.

"My husband will be home tomorrow," Kai said. "He will want to bury his father himself."

The doctor nodded. "I'll be back to check on Aideen tomorrow," he said.

"That was a fine steak, Sam," Murphy said. "Thank you."

They were on the porch with cups of coffee. Murphy smoked his pipe.

"I'll be leaving at eight tomorrow morning to catch the train," Murphy said.

"It doesn't leave until ten," Sam said.

"I'd like to shop for a gift for Kai," Murphy said. "How she puts up with me is anybody's guess."

Sam grinned.

"What?" Murphy said.

"I've heard her say that a time or two," Sam said.

Murphy grinned. "I guess you have at that," he said.

CHAPTER SIXTEEN

After retrieving Boyle from the boxcar, Murphy walked him to the road and mounted the saddle.

"Let's go home, boy," Murphy said.

After six hours in the boxcar, Boyle wanted to run, and Murphy let him. Boyle covered the ten miles to his father's farm in forty-five minutes.

Murphy dismounted at the hitching post. "I'll be back directly," he said to Boyle and walked quickly to the house.

Kai came out and looked at him.

Murphy stopped short. "Something's happened," he said.

Murphy peered down at his father's body in the bed. He appeared to be sleeping.

"Where's my mother?" he said.

"Sedated," Kai said.

"Tell me what happened," Murphy said.

"I've made some coffee," Kai said. "Come to the kitchen."

Murphy followed Kai to the kitchen where she filled two cups with fresh coffee.

"Who did this and why?" Murphy said.

As they drank coffee, Kai told Murphy everything that happened.

"He died to save me from being raped," Kai said. "He was a very brave man, your father. He didn't hesitate for one second to step in, even though he knew he would be shot."

"I'll build him a coffin in the morning," Murphy said. "His brother will need to be notified."

"I'll go to town tomorrow and send him a wire," Kai said.

"Is my mother able to see me?" Murphy said.

Kai nodded.

They went to a bedroom on the second floor. Aideen was in and out of sleep in bed, but she heard Kai and Murphy enter the room and opened her eyes.

"You're home," Aideen said weakly.

Murphy sat on the bed and took Aideen's hand. "I'm home," he said.

Kai fixed a supper of beef stew with fresh bread. Aideen woke up and insisted on eating at the table.

"Kai told you how he died?" Aideen said.

"Yes," Murphy said.

"It was his way to protect those who needed it," Aideen said. "You got that from him, son."

Murphy nodded.

"All the men on the farm are in shock," Aideen said.

"I'll speak to them in the morning," Murphy said.

Aideen nodded. "Kai, would you see me to my room?" she said.

Kai stood and took Aideen's hand.

Murphy watched Kai brush her hair from the bed. She looked at him in the mirror.

"What are you going to do about this?" she said.

"You know damn well what I'm going to do about this," Murphy said.

"I expect no less," Kai said.

In the morning, Murphy built a coffin made of oak and pine.

Then he went to the area reserved for final resting places and dug a grave.

Kai and his father's foreman took the buggy to town. When they returned, the town sheriff rode with them on horseback.

Shirtless, dripping sweat, Murphy met the buggy and sheriff by the porch steps of the house.

"I don't know what to say," the sheriff said as he dismounted.

"I expect you'll want to speak to my mother," Murphy said.

"If I may," the sheriff said.

Murphy looked at Kai and she nodded.

"Come with me, Sheriff," Kai said.

Murphy returned to his digging until the hole was six feet deep and wide enough for the coffin.

Then he sat and looked into the hole he had just dug that would be his father's final resting place.

"Come wash up," Kai said from behind him. "I'm making supper."

"I'll be along in a minute," Murphy said.

"The sheriff asked when the service will be," Kai said.

"I'd best ask the preacher in town," Murphy said. "Tomorrow will do."

"I already asked him," Kai said. "Come in the house now. You must be hungry."

Murphy stood, looked down into the hole, then put his arm around Kai and they walked to the house.

CHAPTER SEVENTEEN

More than one hundred people gathered in the backyard area to bid Michael Murphy farewell and goodbye.

Included in the gathering were all of Michael's hands as well as Murphy's, the doctor and sheriff, Michael's brother and his sons, neighbors from town, and the publisher of the local newspaper.

A dozen women helped Kai and Aideen make lunch for the crowd. People gathered in the house and on the porch.

Murphy pulled the newspaper publisher aside on the porch.

"You employ a sketch artist at the newspaper who does your political cartoons and such?" Murphy said.

"Yes, I do," the publisher said.

"Send him here tomorrow," Murphy said. "I'd like him to make a sketch for me. I'll pay his normal fee."

"All right," the publisher said.

"Thank you," Murphy said.

The sheriff came out to the porch. "There you are, Mr. Murphy," he said. "I want you to know that those two men won't get away with this. They will be hunted by every lawman in the country."

"I'm sure they will be," Murphy said.

"Mr. Murphy, this is a situation for the law," the sheriff said.

"I know," Murphy said.

"I need to get back to town," the sheriff said. "Your father was a good man. He will be missed."

Murphy watched the sheriff walk to his horse. He noticed a buggy on the road. Driving the buggy was Burke.

Murphy waited for Burke to arrive on the porch.

"I came as soon as I got word," Burke said.

"Kai sent you a telegram?" Murphy said.

"She did."

"Come in," Murphy said.

After everyone had left, Murphy and Burke sat in chairs on the porch with glasses of whiskey. Burke smoked a cigar, Murphy his pipe.

"There is no need for me to guess what you're going to do about this," Burke said.

"And what am I going to do about this?" Murphy said.

"Hunt them down," Burke said. "No matter where they go or how long it takes, you'll hunt them down."

Murphy took a sip of bourbon and then puffed on his pipe.

"I spoke to Arthur," Burke said. "He said you are to act within your powers as a secret service agent. Therefore, he has had a federal warrant for those two men issued. I have it in my pocket."

Burke reached into his jacket pocket for the warrant and handed it to Murphy. "Fill in their names before you show it," he said. "We didn't know them at the time the warrant was issued."

"Tell Arthur he has my thanks," Murphy said.

Burke nodded.

"And you have my thanks as well," Murphy said.

"We've worked together for a while now, Murphy," Burke said. "If you need anything, don't hesitate to call."

"Are you going back to Washington?" Murphy said.

"Tomorrow," Burke said.

"If you can, keep track of Grant," Murphy said. "He hasn't

much time."

Burke nodded.

"Shall we have another drink?" Burke said.

Chapter Eighteen

After breakfast, Burke took his buggy back to town. An hour or so later, the cartoonist for the local newspaper arrived.

Named Hans Fritz, he was a German immigrant who came to America during the Civil War to sketch photographs of the battles. After the war, he stayed and found he could make a decent living drawing for newspapers and magazines. He even created covers for dime novels.

Murphy met Fritz on the porch and brought him into the house. Kai and Aideen were in the living room. The baby was asleep in her basket on the coffee table.

"Mr. Fritz, this is my mother, Aideen, and my wife, Kai," Murphy said. "Mother, Kai, Mr. Fritz is a sketch artist from the newspaper. With your help, he's going to draw a picture of the two men who killed Father."

"Where is the lighting best?" Fritz said.

"On the porch this time of day," Aideen said.

"I'll get my pad," Fritz said.

The sketch of Moats took about three hours to complete, but when it was done it was a remarkable likeness.

They all took a break for lunch, then continued the job on the back porch, as the light had shifted.

By four o'clock, the sketch of Holland was complete.

Murphy saw Fritz to his buggy.

"Mr. Fritz, please keep this between us," Murphy said and handed Fritz an envelope with one thousand dollars in it.

Fritz looked at the envelope. "Yes, sir, Mr. Murphy," he said. "Between us."

Before supper, Murphy went to Michael's den. His father had kept meticulous records on everything, including the men he'd hired.

Murphy went through his father's record book of the men he employed. Moats was thirty-four years old and claimed to be from Little Rock, Arkansas. Holland gave his age as thirty-six and came from Oklahoma Territory.

They both claimed to be living in Texas before moving to Tennessee to work on the farm. They claimed to have worked on a cattle ranch south of Austin for a man named Joe Bass.

After supper, Murphy and Kai took coffee on the porch.

"Did you see what kind of horses they rode?" Murphy said.

"Moats rode a brown bay with a white star in the center of his muzzle," Kai said. "Holland rode a paint bay."

There was no need to ask Kai if she was sure about the horses. The years she'd spent living with the Sioux and Navajo had honed her senses to a razor sharp point.

"When will you go?" Kai said.

"Day after tomorrow."

"I will go with you," Kai said.

"No, you will not," Murphy said.

"Do you forget I lived with the Sioux and Navajo?" Kai said. "I am no little doll of a woman, Murphy."

"Kai, what I have to do is to deal with the very worst of white man," Murphy said. "And I need you here to watch over my mother while I am gone. With you gone, I'm afraid dealing with the farms and my father's murder will be too much for her to bear at this time."

From inside the house, the baby cried.

"And then there is that," Murphy said.

71

Kai nodded. "You are right, of course," she said. "I'd best tend to the baby."

"I'll be in directly," Murphy said.

The sun was setting, and the porch was growing dark. Murphy lit his pipe and watched the sun sink lower until it was gone.

Kai returned with two cups of fresh coffee, set them on the table, and then lit the porch lantern.

"Aideen and the baby are asleep," Kai said.

"I will see to it the foremen run the farms while I'm away, but my mother will need you," Murphy said. "They were married for nearly fifty years. It's going to be hard on her once the initial shock has worn off."

"She is strong, but I will see to her, so don't worry," Kai said. "The baby is asleep. Let's go to bed."

In the dark, Kai rested her head against Murphy's naked chest.

"They were going to rape me," Kai said. "And to save my honor, your father gave his life. Without hesitation. What he didn't know is that I would have allowed myself to be violated to save his and Aideen's lives."

Murphy held Kai tight against his chest.

"Do not kill these men," Kai said. "Bring them to Fort Smith so I can watch them hang in Judge Parker's court. Promise me that."

"I promise," Murphy said.

CHAPTER NINETEEN

trimming his beard, Murphy took a hot bath. He dressed
trail clothes before breakfast.

had packed his saddlebags with extra trail clothes,
ear, socks, ammunition for the Colt and Winchester, and
ks of Michael's whiskey.

fast was a feast of eggs, bacon, potatoes, biscuits, and

Aideen walked Murphy to the porch, where the fore-
le to the hitching post.

hat and holster. Murphy took the hat and
ded her right hand and Murphy took

transformation a hundred times
her. As the holster went on,
olaced by a coiled, very

e change. Aideen's

Murphy said.

mounted the

he baby a bath, dressed

her, and put her in the basket for a nap.

Aideen made some Earl Grey tea and they sat at the table with cups and thin biscuits.

"Kai, my son seemed so different this morning when he put on his holster," Aideen said. "You must have noticed it as well."

"Many times," Kai said.

"That name you called him that day on the porch, what was it?" Aideen said.

"Regulator," Kai said.

"What does it mean?" Aideen said.

"Murphy works directly for the president," Kai said. "He is authorized to carry out orders for the president. He uses any means possible to regulate the law."

Aideen stared at Kai for a long moment. "Any means possible?" she said.

Kai nodded.

"No wonder you took a shotgun to Burke," Aideen said.

Kai grinned at the memory. "Yeah," she said. "No wonde

The ten o'clock train stopped in Dallas for two hours proceeding to Austin, extending the traveling time to hours.

Murphy reserved a sleeping car, although how mu he would do was questionable.

Before boarding the train, he stopped at t withdrew two thousand dollars for expenses. H tions with Kai to deposit the check coming fror the bank when it arrived.

The farm and whiskey business, under his leave his mother a wealthy woman. Kai, too

His mother would enter into old age but Murphy knew she would trade all father back. So would he. A man can

but once your father was gone, he was gone.

Murphy skipped lunch, substituting a nap for the meal. He awoke in time for dinner and ate a hearty steak in the dining car. Having nothing to do after dinner, he went to the gentlemen's car to kill some time.

The car was crowded. Murphy ordered a bourbon at the bar and found a seat by a window. Six men were engaged in a heated card game at a center table. One man had a pretty young woman standing by his side. He appeared to be her father.

"My dear, would you bring me a coffee from the bar," the man said.

The young woman went to the bar for the coffee. As she returned to the table, she tripped and spilled hot coffee on the man opposite her father. The scalded man jumped to his feet.

"Oh, my goodness, I am so sorry," the girl said. "I'll get you a towel."

The girl ran to the bar, returned with a towel, and dabbed at the man's wet shirt. "Please forgive me, sir," the girl said.

And while all eyes were on the young girl toweling dry the man's shirt, her father palmed himself a winning hand.

"I think that's satisfactory," the man with the wet shirt said. "Let's finish the hand."

After calling and raising, the "father" won a very large pot.

"Well, that's it for me," the man with the wet shirt said.

"Not so fast," Murphy said as he stood up and walked to the table.

All eyes went to Murphy. "One thing I can't abide is a man cheating at cards," Murphy said.

"Who, sir, is cheating?" the man with the wet shirt said.

"Him," Murphy said and tapped the "father" on the shoulder.

"I resent that remark, sir," the "father" said.

Murphy grabbed the man's right arm, shook it, and several aces and kings fell out of his sleeve.

"One of you men go for the railroad police officer," Murphy said. "He should be in the first riding car. I'll hold onto this gentleman until he gets here."

In Dallas, Murphy got off the train to stretch his legs. On the platform, the man with the wet shirt approached Murphy.

"I never did thank you, sir," the man said. "You saved me a great deal of money."

"Never play cards with a man who has a daughter or a wife bringing him drinks," Murphy said. "You're sure to get spilled on."

"I will remember that, sir," the man said. "And good night to you."

After the man left the platform, Murphy went to the boxcar to visit Boyle. The large horse was happy to see Murphy. As Murphy brushed Boyle, he fed him some sugar cubes he'd taken from the dining car.

"We'll be in Austin around four in the morning," Murphy said. "I'll find you a nice livery where you can get some sleep."

Murphy returned to his sleeping car where he poured a small drink of bourbon and smoked his pipe.

His father was gone. A man of peace his entire life had died a violent death to preserve the honor of his daughter-in-law.

Growing up, his father never laid a hand upon him, even when he deserved it. He never spoke crossly to Aideen—or anybody else, for that matter. He believed in hard work and self-reliance and had built his whiskey business from nothing but a dream and a spring of fresh water.

Michael offered any man of any color or religion a job at a good wage, if he was willing to work. To be murdered by two men to whom he gave jobs couldn't and wouldn't stand.

The slowing of the train alerted Murphy that they had arrived in Austin. He gathered up his saddlebags, left the sleeping car, and waited for the train to stop and the doors to open.

Austin, the capital of Texas, was a thriving city of twelve thousand residents.

After bringing Boyle out of the boxcar, Murphy stood on a dark street and looked at a thousand lanterns illuminating the sidewalks.

"Come on, boy, let's find that hotel we stayed at once before," Murphy said.

Holding the reins, Murphy walked Boyle into downtown Austin to Front Street and the Doral Hotel, a four-story structure that had its own livery.

Murphy tied Boyle to the hitching post and entered the grand lobby. A sleepy-eyed clerk sat behind the desk.

"Just get off the train?" the clerk said.

Murphy nodded. "I need a room and a stable for my horse," he said.

"How many nights?"

"Two or more," Murphy said.

"Five dollars a night, two for the horse," the clerk said. "In advance."

Murphy gave the clerk twenty-four dollars. "I'll see to my horse and be back for the room key," he said.

After tending to Boyle in the stable, Murphy carried his saddlebags up to his room on the fourth floor. The large room had a balcony. He poured two ounces of bourbon from his flask into a water glass, lit his pipe, and sat in a chair on the balcony. From there he looked at Austin below.

The sun would be up soon. Town workers were extinguishing the lanterns along the sidewalks. Off in the distance, he could see the capitol building.

He felt weary, and his journey had barely begun. He sighed and watched the sunrise, then grabbed a few hours of sleep.

CHAPTER TWENTY

Although firearms weren't banned in Austin, Murphy didn't see another man wearing one. He drew stares from people on the street as he walked to the sheriff's office from the hotel.

The sheriff's department in Austin was a large operation. Besides the sheriff, twenty deputies worked round the clock keeping the peace.

Sheriff Jake Schram was in his private office at the sheriff's department. He was a weathered man of around fifty. A deputy escorted Murphy into Schram's office.

Murphy presented his identification.

"US Secret Service? Is the president coming?" Schram said.

"I'm here to see a rancher named Joe Bass," Murphy said. "Know him?"

"Everybody within a hundred square miles knows Joe Bass," Schram said. "What's your business with him?"

"I have a warrant issued by the Justice Department in Washington for the arrest of two men who once worked for him," Murphy said. "At present I don't know where the two men are. I was hoping his hands might recall any places the two men were fond of or spoke of in passing."

"May I see the warrant?" Schram said.

Murphy removed the warrant from his jacket pocket and handed it to Schram. "The names don't look familiar," he said and returned the warrant to Murphy.

"Can you direct me to the Bass ranch?" Murphy said.

"As my ass is sore from sitting in this chair, I'll ride you out there myself," Schram said.

"I'll get my horse," Murphy said.

The ride south to the Bass ranch took about an hour.

Joe Bass was a tough old bird of about sixty, a man who had buried two wives, raised three sons and one daughter. He'd scratched and clawed for everything he had. He was a good rancher and paid a fair wage for a fair day's work. He employed an exceptional cook for the men, as he believed a man worked better with a proper diet.

Bass knew Schram well and invited him and Murphy to talk over lunch. They dined in the backyard of his ranch house at a table under a shady tree.

Steak was prepared on a backyard pit by a cook.

"When I came here forty years ago, Austin was nothing but a settlement," Bass said. "I fought Comanche, drought, rustlers, thieves, and every pox known to man. I buried two wives and almost died myself on several occasions. Texas was a slave state back then, but I never once bought or sold human flesh. I tell you all this for one reason. The thing I have come to hate most in this world is a cattle thief."

"Are you trying to tell me Moats and Holland were cattle thieves?" Murphy said.

"I couldn't prove it," Bass said. "If I could, I would have hung them both."

"Is that why they quit?" Murphy said. "Because you suspected them?"

"I didn't ask them," Schram said. "I just gave them their pay, and they rode out. I was glad to be rid of them."

"How many hands do you have?" Murphy said.

"My foreman and twelve," Bass said. "Plus my three sons. Come time for a drive, I bring in another eight or so."

"What time do the hands come in for the night?" Murphy said.

"Evening chow is at six," Bass said.

"Can I speak to your men?" Murphy said.

"Why don't you ride with me to the north range," Bass said. "By the time we get back, all hands should be in the bunkhouse."

"I'll take my leave," Schram said. "I have business in town."

"Good day, Sheriff," Bass said. "Always good to see you."

The north range consisted of several thousand square acres of land on which two thousand head of cattle grazed. Four cowboys tended to the herd.

"Ever work cattle, Mr. Murphy?' Bass said.

"Some," Murphy said.

"North or south?" Bass said.

"North. I rode with Grant for the most part," Murphy said.

"I'm from Rhode Island myself," Bass said. "Never had any use for slavery. I was forced to sell beef to the Confederacy by Davis and Lee, but I was glad the North won."

"How many head to do you run?" Murphy said.

"Near eleven thousand," Bass said. "Moats and Holland, what did they do to deserve a federal warrant delivered by a secret service agent?"

"Cold-blooded murder," Murphy said.

"I guess it's not much of a stretch to go from cattle theft to murder," Bass said. "Let's go back and have a cool drink while we wait for the men."

"Sounds good," Murphy said.

Bass and Murphy sat in chairs on the front porch. Each had a glass filled with six ounces of water and two ounces of bourbon whiskey. Murphy smoked his pipe, while Bass smoked a cigar.

"I see some of the hands riding in now," Bass said. "Once

they're all in, we'll go down and you can have a talk with them."

Fifteen minutes later, Bass and Murphy walked into the bunkhouse where a dozen hands were sitting down to supper.

"Men, I need to delay your supper for a few minutes," Bass said. "This is Mr. Murphy. He is a US secret service agent and has a few questions about a pair of hands who worked here maybe five months ago. Moats and Holland."

Murphy looked at the dozen men at the table. His eyes locked onto a young hand at the end of the table.

"Ned Roberts?" Murphy said.

"I didn't think you'd remember me," Roberts said.

"You know this man?" Bass said.

"Worked on my father's farm for about a year," Murphy said. "Ned, what are you doing here?"

"I'm from Austin," Roberts said. "Guess I got homesick."

"Can we talk outside for a few minutes?" Murphy said.

"Sure."

On the porch of the bunkhouse, Murphy said, "Moats and Holland. I have a warrant for their arrest. Murder. Did you ever talk to them about my father and his whiskey?"

"In passing," Roberts said. "Around the dinner table. I told everybody about making whiskey and such. It was just talk, is all."

"Thanks for the information, Ned," Murphy said.

"Who did they murder?" Roberts said.

"My father," Murphy said.

On the porch of his house, Bass said, "Stay for supper, Mr. Murphy?"

"I best head back before dark," Murphy said.

"Mr. Murphy, I'm sorry about your father," Bass said.

"Bunkhouse talk," Murphy said. "Roberts told them he worked for a rich whiskey maker, and they headed to Tennessee with the idea of robbing him."

"I hope you catch them," Bass said. "They deserve hanging."

"Yes, they do," Murphy said.

CHAPTER TWENTY-ONE

After having supper in his room, Murphy sat in the chair on the balcony with a glass of whiskey and his pipe and watched the city of Austin go to sleep for the night.

Lanterns began lighting up all across the city as darkness set in.

So now he knew how and why Holland and Moats came to work for his father. They had planned all along to rob him. They waited for the opportunity to present itself. When it did, they acted.

He learned why they went to his father, but he didn't learn where they went after they killed him.

There was a soft knock on the door. Murphy stood and went to the door. "Yes?" he said.

"Mr. Murphy?" a male voice said.

"Yes."

"My name is Gale, sir. I am a Texas Ranger. May I have a moment of your time?"

Murphy opened the door. Gale was a stout man of medium height.

"Mr. Murphy, the chief would like to speak with you in the morning," Gale said.

"What about?" Murphy said.

"I wasn't told," Gale said. "Just that it was a matter of official business."

"What time?" Murphy said.

"Ten o'clock," Gale said. "I am to escort you to Texas Rangers' headquarters."

"I'll be in the lobby at ten o'clock," Murphy said.

"Good night, sir," Gale said.

Murphy closed the door and returned to the balcony.

The chief of the Texas Rangers was the highest law enforcement authority in the state and answered directly to the governor. With him in his office was a captain, who served as his aide.

The captain offered freshly brewed coffee to Murphy.

"When I bumped into Schram on the street yesterday afternoon and he told me a secret service agent was in town, do you know what my first thought was?" the chief said.

"The president was coming," Murphy said.

"You've heard that before," the chief said.

"A time or two," Murphy said.

"It is my understanding the secret service deals with counterfeit money," the chief said.

"That is one of its functions," Murphy said.

The chief nodded to the captain, who produced a thin stack of bills and handed them to Murphy.

"The Bank of Austin notified us of what they believe are counterfeit twenty-dollar bills," the chief said.

Murphy glanced at the bills. "They are counterfeit, all right," he said.

"You barely looked at them," the chief said.

"The ink is too green and still wet, the borders are offset, the seal is the wrong color brown, and the printing press they used lacked the weight to press the bill properly," Murphy said. "The fibers are wrong. If you set fire to this bill, it would go up in a puff of smoke rather than a slow burn."

"You got all that from a glance?" the chief said.

"A glance and fifteen years' experience of looking at

counterfeit money," Murphy said.

The chief shrugged. "Right," he said.

"Suppose you tell me how you came by these bills?" Murphy said.

"About three months ago a man named William Cutler came to Austin and opened a print shop," the chief said. "We think the bills came from his shop."

"This Cutler, what does he look like?" Murphy said.

"Small fellow, around sixty. Wears round eyeglasses," the chief said.

"Where's his shop?" Murphy said.

Murphy and the chief arrived at the print shop in the chief's carriage.

"Are you sure you don't want some of my men with us?" the chief said.

"We're fine," Murphy said.

The chief told his driver to wait for them. Then he and Murphy stepped down from the carriage.

They entered the print shop. It was cluttered with paper, ink, a press, and printing blocks. No one was at the counter. A bell sat on the counter. Murphy picked it up and rang it.

A door to a back room opened, and a small man wearing glasses stepped out and went to the counter.

"Hello, Artie," Murphy said. "When did you get out?"

"Artie?" the chief said.

"Artie Jones," Murphy said.

Artie looked at Murphy. "Goddammit it all to hell," Artie said. "Of all the print shops in the world you could have walked into, you have to walk into mine."

"How have you been, Artie?" Murphy said. "Prison treat you all right?"

"Oh, you know," Artie said.

"Mind if I take a look in the back?" Murphy said.

"Do I have a choice?" Artie said.

"No."

Artie led Murphy and the chief into the back room where a press for printing money was centered. A station for printing ink sat against the wall. An engraving station was against another wall.

"Still do your own engraving?" Murphy said.

"Don't insult me," Artie said.

Murphy looked at the chief. "Artie worked for the mint as an engraver," he said.

"Twenty goddam years," Artie said. "For thirty-two dollars a week."

"Until one day he went into business for himself," Murphy said. "Until one day about eight years ago, I arrested him."

"Damn you, Murphy," Artie said. "And a fellow Irishman at that."

"I thought you got fifteen years," Murphy said.

"I made parole on account of I turned sixty, and they didn't want me to die in prison," Artie said.

"I have bad news for you, Artie," Murphy said.

"Oh, goddammit," Artie said.

Murphy and the chief sat at a table in the Scoot Inn, a saloon that opened in 1871. They had glasses of whiskey. Murphy smoked his pipe.

"If those two men show their noses in Texas, I'll have every ranger on alert," the chief said.

"Appreciate it," Murphy said. "Now about this hooplehead Jones. I don't have time to take him to Washington."

"What do you propose?" the chief said.

"Offer him a job," Murphy said.

★ ★ ★ ★ ★

Murphy and the chief met with Artie at the jail. A deputy brought Artie to the interview room.

"They won't let me have any goddamn coffee," Artie said.

Murphy looked at the deputy. "Bring him coffee," he said.

The deputy nodded and left the room.

"Artie, the chief has something to tell you. I advise you to listen carefully," Murphy said.

"What are my options?" Artie said.

"Die in prison," Murphy said.

"I'm all ears," Artie said.

"You can spend the rest of your life in prison, or you can go straight," the chief said. "Run your print shop legitimately. You can print posters for the rangers. I can get you a dozen accounts with saloons and restaurants for menus. What's it going to be, Mr. Jones? Prison or legitimate?"

Artie looked at Murphy. "It beats busting rocks," Murphy said.

"I guess I'm going straight," Artie said.

CHAPTER TWENTY-TWO

Before catching the train, Murphy had breakfast at the hotel with the chief and Sheriff Schram.

"Mr. Murphy, if Holland and Moats are in Texas, we'll find them for you," the chief said.

"If they do show up, hold them and wire me in Washington at the White House, or in Fort Smith in care of Judge Parker," Murphy said. "Either way, I'll get it."

"Where you headed?' Schram said.

"Little Rock," Murphy said.

The ten o'clock train to Little Rock had one layover. It was scheduled to arrive in Little Rock at one in the morning.

Murphy paid for a sleeping car so he could nap or read in private. After settling Boyle into the boxcar, Murphy boarded the train and went to his sleeping car.

Before breakfast, he sent a telegram to Kai and his mother. The sleeping car, besides a bed, contained a desk and a comfortable chair. Murphy poured two ounces of bourbon from his flask into a water glass, lit his pipe, and sat in the chair to read the Austin newspaper.

A political story on Cleveland occupied most of page one. He was distancing himself from the pack and was predicted to emerge as the favorite to win the nomination.

Through with the newspaper, Murphy dug out the book he'd stored in his saddlebags and opened it to where he had left off.

The book was a novel by the famed Russian author Tolstoy, titled *The Cossacks*.

The novel was a short read, and Murphy raced through it in a few hours. When he closed the book, he put on his jacket and went to the gentlemen's car to occupy his mind.

He wasn't ready to think about his father just yet. An occupied mind didn't have time to think about hardships, loneliness, or home. It was a trick he'd learned during the war. Before he rose through the ranks when he was an enlisted man, there was a great deal of downtime between battles. Weeks would pass, sometimes even months, between engagements. Time was spent marching and drilling, but that wasn't enough to occupy a man's mind. If you let it, your mind focused on the fact that in the next battle your life might end. Thinking about the possibility of your own demise in battle was enough to drive a man over the edge. More men deserted in downtime than during battle due to an excess of thinking.

So he found ways to occupy his mind. Reading, writing letters, even keeping a journal; everything and anything to keep his focus from death.

Murphy ordered a small bourbon at the bar and found a vacant seat by a window. The scenery rolled by at an astounding fifty miles an hour, some fifteen miles faster than the fastest horse.

"Do you play?" a man said.

"Excuse me?" Murphy said.

"You are seated at the chess table. Do you play?" the man said.

"I do," Murphy said.

"Feel like a game?" the man said.

"Why not?" Murphy said.

"I'll get the pieces," the man said.

The board was carved into the table. The man returned with

a wood box containing the pieces.

"Shall we toss a coin for the color?" the man said.

Murphy produced a silver dollar, flipped it, caught it, and slapped it on the table under his hand. "Call it," he said.

"Heads I play white," the man said.

Murphy removed his hand. The coin was heads. "Black to me," Murphy said.

They set up the board. The man made the first move. "I'm in farming supplies," the man said. "I travel as far west as Kansas. May I ask what line you're in?"

"Whiskey," Murphy said. "My father and I make our own brand of bourbon."

"Really? Have you a sample?" the man said.

Murphy moved his rook, then stood and went to the bar for two empty glasses. He returned, took out his flask, and added an ounce to each glass. Murphy and the man each took a small sip and the man said, "Outstanding, sir. What do you call it?"

"Murphy's," Murphy said.

"I shall remember it," the man said.

The game lasted two hours and ended in a draw.

"Good game, sir," the man said. "And I will remember your whiskey."

Murphy returned to his sleeping car and took a short nap. He awoke refreshed and hungry, as he had skipped lunch.

He washed his hands in the washbasin and combed his hair, tossed on his jacket, and went to the dining car. The man he had played chess with sat alone at a table. He waved to Murphy. "Please join me, Mr. Murphy," he said.

Murphy took a chair at the man's table.

"I ordered the baked chicken," the man said. "I'm told it's quite good."

Murphy ordered the same.

"I neglected to give you my name," the man said. "It's Horace

Hastings, but most people call me Harry."

"Where are you traveling to, Harry?" Murphy said.

"Little Rock first," Harry said. "Then to Fort Smith, and then as far west as Kansas."

"I will be in Little Rock for a few days myself," Murphy said. "Maybe we can have dinner together one night and play another game of chess."

"I would like that," Harry said.

Harry, who stood around five-foot-five, looked up at Boyle as he walked with Murphy down the ramp to the street.

"That is quite a horse, Murphy," Harry said. "But I suppose a man your size needs a large horse."

"Where are you staying?" Murphy said.

"The Hotel Little Rock on Main Street," Harry said. "They have a livery."

"Lead the way," Murphy said.

The Hotel Little Rock was a six-story structure with balconies on the fifth and sixth floors. Harry didn't like heights and chose a room on the first floor. Murphy picked a room on the sixth floor.

After settling into his room, Murphy dug out the second flask and poured a few ounces into a water glass and took his pipe to the balcony. As with Austin, the dark streets of Little Rock were illuminated by thousands of street lanterns.

Murphy sipped his drink and smoked his pipe while watching the pinpricks of lights below twinkle like tiny stars.

Drink finished, Murphy went to bed.

CHAPTER TWENTY-THREE

Little Rock was a sprawling town of fifteen thousand residents. Built on the banks of the Arkansas River, Little Rock was a port town of great importance. Surrounded by farms and ranches, ships arrived and departed daily.

Little Rock was a blend of rough and tumble teamsters, cowboys, farmers, and shopkeepers. The streets were crowded with wagons, buggies, cowboys, and pedestrians.

Murphy found the sheriff's office on Front Street. The sheriff sat behind his desk.

"Can I help you?" he said.

Murphy handed the sheriff his identification.

"Is the president coming?" the sheriff said.

"No," Murphy said. "I have a federal warrant issued by the Justice Department for John Moats and Tom Holland. Moats comes from a farm or ranch near Little Rock. Can you tell me where I could find it?"

"Personally, no," the sheriff said. "I've only recently been elected. Some of my deputies might know."

"Where can I find your deputies?" Murphy said.

"At the moment, five are scattered all over town," the sheriff said. "At four o'clock they report here, and another five work until midnight. Then two come on at midnight and work until eight."

"At four o'clock, ten of your deputies will be in your office?" Murphy said.

"Yes. You can ask them then," the sheriff said.

"Fair enough," Murphy said.

Murphy returned to the hotel livery and gave Boyle a good brushing. "Want to go for a ride, boy?" he said.

After being cooped up on trains and in stables, Boyle did not want to walk or trot but run. Murphy let him go for about ten miles to the east. He slowed Boyle to walk along the banks of the Arkansas River.

Murphy walked Boyle to the shade of a tree, removed the saddle, and gave the massive horse a good brushing. Boyle munched on grass as Murphy worked the brush.

"We seem to have a problem retiring," Murphy said as he ran the brush along Boyle's back. "Something, it seems, always calls us back."

After brushing Boyle, Murphy sat with his back against the saddle, smoked his pipe, and watched a barge sail along the river.

Boyle stayed close by and munched on grass.

After a while, Murphy looked at his watch. "Time to go, boy," he said.

"Men, this is Secret Service Agent Murphy," the sheriff said. "He has a federal warrant for the arrest of John Moats. He wants to know if any of you are familiar with the Moats family."

"I know that prick, John Moats," a deputy said. "His whole family is a bunch of mean bastards. They come to town only maybe three times a year, but they're trouble."

"How so?" Murphy said.

"Well, there's three brothers, one sister, and their ma," the deputy said. "The brothers are as mean-spirited as any men I ever met. The sister is . . . well, trouble all by herself."

"And John Moats?" Murphy said.

"He was the oldest," the deputy said. "He left a few years ago to work on a cattle ranch in Texas, I heard."

"How do I get to their place?" Murphy said.

"I can have three deputies ride you out there in the morning," the sheriff said.

"Three?" Murphy said.

"You'll want the company," the sheriff said.

Before going to dinner, Murphy checked for Harry at the hotel, but he wasn't in. Murphy ate at the hotel restaurant and decided to walk around town afterward. Many of the men wore sidearms, and Murphy wore his.

He walked through town and turned down a side street lined with eleven saloons. Laughter and music echoed loudly on the entire block.

As he passed one saloon called the Lady Gay, Murphy heard a familiar voice cry out, "I meant no offense. It was an accident."

Murphy peered over the swinging doors. Two cowboys held Harry by the arms while a third cowboy poured whiskey over his head.

Murphy pushed in the door and walked over to the bar and the cowboy pouring whiskey over Harry's head. He drew his Colt and stuck it in the man's back.

"That's enough, friend," Murphy said. "Put down the bottle, or I'll put a hole in your back large enough to fit a wagon wheel through."

The cowboy set the bottle on the bar.

"Turn around," Murphy said.

The cowboy turned and looked up at Murphy. Murphy smacked him across the head with the heavy Colt, knocking him unconscious to the floor.

Murphy holstered the Colt and looked at Harry. "Duck,"

Murphy said.

Harry put his head down and Murphy punched both cowboys in the face, knocking them to the floor.

Murphy looked at the sixty or so men seated at tables. "What's the matter with you men?" he said. "You sit here and watch three men beat up on a harmless salesman and don't do anything."

Every man stared silently at Murphy. "Come on, Harry. Let's go back to the hotel," Murphy said.

Murphy and Harry met in the hotel restaurant for dinner after Harry changed his shirt and suit.

"The way you handled those men, you're no ordinary whiskey maker, Mr. Murphy," Harry said.

"What brought that ruckus on, Harry?" Murphy said.

"I stepped on his foot," Harry said. "I didn't see him and stepped on his foot. It was an accident and, well, you saw the rest."

"Do me a favor, Harry. Stay out of saloons," Murphy said.

CHAPTER TWENTY-FOUR

Murphy met the sheriff and three of his deputies in front of the sheriff's office after breakfast.

"My men will ride with you to the Moats place," the sheriff said. "And from what they tell me, you'd best be careful and watch your back."

"Appreciate the assistance, Sheriff," Murphy said.

The ride south to the Moats ranch took about ninety minutes.

"That's their property there," a deputy said, pointing.

The house was a large shack, the corral in serious need of repair, and the barn was barely standing.

"Not much to look at, is it?" a deputy said.

They rode to the porch and waited. Three men with shotguns and a woman with a rifle came out to the porch. The three men wore long-sleeved undershirts. The woman wore a dress and was barefoot.

One of the three men said, "This here be private property, and you be trespassing. Leave or get shot."

"My name is . . ." Murphy said.

"Don't care what your name is," the man said. "Leave or get shot."

"Then you'd best shoot," Murphy said.

"What?" the man said.

"I said, then you'd best shoot," Murphy said.

The man stared at Murphy, a bit confused.

"But before you do, know this," Murphy said. He drew his

Colt in the blink of an eye. "I'll get two of you, possibly three, before that woman with the rifle gets me. Are two or three of you willing to die right here, right now, rather than hear what I have to say?"

The door opened and a woman of about sixty walked out to the porch. "No, they ain't," she said. "Jeb, you and your brothers put down them guns. Maybelle, you too."

The three men and the woman lowered their weapons.

Murphy holstered his Colt. "Are you Mrs. Moats?" he said.

"I am. Name is Louise but I answer to Lou. Who you be?"

"Name is Murphy."

"State your business, Murphy," Lou said.

"I'm a United States secret service agent," Murphy said.

"We pay our taxes every year on time," Lou said. "We got no quarrel with you revenue folks."

"I'm not a tax collector. I'm a lawman," Murphy said. "I'm here about your son John."

"Step down. Come on the porch. Maybelle, fetch us the coffeepot," Lou said. "You other three can join us."

A few minutes later, Murphy, the deputies, Lou, her sons, and Maybelle all had cups of coffee on the porch. Only Murphy and Lou sat in chairs.

Lou lit a cigar and said, "My boy John ain't been home in years. What's he done that the law is after him?"

"Robbery and murder," Murphy said.

Lou sighed heavily. "John always was no good," she said. "Not like my three boys here. I always knew John would come to murder."

"Mrs. Moats, would—" Murphy said.

"Lou."

"Lou, would you have any idea where John might go if he needed to hide?" Murphy said.

"John hasn't been home in years," Lou said. "I know he went

97

to Texas some time ago, but he never wrote, not once. If he's running from the law, he could be anywhere. The one place I know he ain't is here."

"You make good coffee, Lou," Murphy said.

"I thank you kindly," Lou said.

"How do we know they're not lying?" a deputy said.

"Moats rides a brown bay with a white star," Murphy said. "Holland rides a paint. I saw neither in the corral."

"They wouldn't give up their own just because you asked," a deputy said.

"No, but I'd be able to tell if they were lying," Murphy said. "And they weren't."

"So what now?" a deputy said.

"I'll try the Hollands in Oklahoma," Murphy said.

Murphy found Harry in his room.

"I see you're packing," Murphy said.

"My business here has concluded my trip," Harry said. "It went quite well, except for that incident in the saloon."

"Where next?" Murphy said.

"Fort Smith."

"Tomorrow?"

"Ten o'clock train."

"We'll ride together then," Murphy said.

"Then we'll play another game of chess," Harry said.

"See you for dinner," Murphy said.

After leaving Harry, Murphy went to the telegraph office where he sent a telegram to Kai and Aideen and another to Judge Parker.

CHAPTER TWENTY-FIVE

Kai met with the foreman in the warehouse.

"There's one hundred barrels ready to be shipped," the foreman said. "Another one hundred ready for the warehouse. What do you wish me to do?"

"Tomorrow, you and I will go to town and make arrangements with the freight company," Kai said. "I'll see to the bottling company and bank while we're there."

"Yes, Mrs. Murphy," the foreman said.

"May I ask a favor?" Kai said.

"Ask."

"Have my horse saddled and bring him to the house," Kai said.

"Sure thing."

Kai returned to the house, where she found Aideen and the baby in the living room.

"Aideen, can you watch the baby until I return?" Kai said. "I'm riding to my husband's farm to check on things."

"Alone?" Aideen said.

"It's only a few miles," Kai said.

Kai went to her bedroom to change into riding pants and shirt, hat, and boots. She removed the .32 caliber revolver Murphy gave her and dropped it in her purse, then returned to the living room.

"Aideen, I'll be back in a few hours," Kai said.

The foreman had her horse at the hitching post. "Mrs.

Murphy, you're wearing pants," he said.

Kai expertly got into the saddle and took the reins from the foreman. "I was riding bareback with the Sioux and Navajo before you were born," she said with a wink.

"Yes, ma'am," the foreman said.

Kai rode to the stream, which was high this time of year, crossed it easily, and continued on to Murphy's property. The ride was easy, just a few miles. As she neared the fields, she could see tall stalks of corn ready for harvest.

She reached the road leading to the house. Workers in the field paused to look at her. At the house, she dismounted and tied her horse to the hitching post. Then she walked down to the barn where the assistant foreman was checking the stock of corn.

"Mrs. Murphy," the assistant foreman said.

"How is the stock?" Kai said.

"Close to maximum," the assistant foreman said.

"We're bringing a hundred barrels to town in a few days, and we'll need to replenish the stock," Kai said.

"Yes, ma'am," the assistant foreman said. "I'll make the arrangements."

"Let's go to the house, and I'll make a pot of coffee," Kai said.

Kai and the assistant foreman drank coffee as they reviewed paperwork in the office.

"These estimates are correct?" Kai said.

"Yes, ma'am," the assistant foreman said.

"Mr. Murphy wanted six hundred barrels this season," Kai said. "I think we can give them to him."

"I'm sure we can," the assistant foreman said. "I can't tell you how sorry I am about Mr. Murphy. He was always a gentleman."

"We all feel that way," Kai said.

"When are you coming home?" the assistant foreman said.

"When Murphy returns with those two sons of bitches in tow," Kai said.

"Yes, ma'am," the assistant foreman said.

Aideen found Kai in the office, where she was pouring over the books.

"There you are," Aiden said. "Supper is just about ready."

"Michael kept meticulous records," Kai said.

"He always did," Aideen said.

"You are a wealthy woman, Aideen," Kai said. "I'm surprised those two murderous bastards didn't ask for more."

"Never mind that now. Come have supper," Aideen said.

After the ten o'clock feeding, Kai put the baby to sleep in her bed. Then she went to check on Aideen.

Aideen was brushing her hair in front of the dresser's mirror.

"Is she asleep?" Aideen said.

"Yes," Kai said. She took the brush from Aideen and brushed her hair.

"Michael would do that for me sometimes," Aideen said. "He loved my hair so."

"I'll braid it for you tomorrow," Kai said.

"My son married well," Aideen said.

CHAPTER TWENTY-SIX

Murphy walked Boyle through the streets of Fort Smith. Harry walked beside Murphy. Several men nodded to Murphy as they walked past.

"People know you here," Harry said.

"I live here," Murphy said. "At least six months out of the year."

"Where do you live the other six?"

"Tennessee," Murphy said. "We'll stay in town tonight. I'm sure you have business to conduct tomorrow."

"There are three large general stores and two feed and grain that sell farm equipment," Harry said.

"That's tomorrow," Murphy said. "Tonight we'll have dinner with a friend of mine."

After checking into the Hotel Fort Smith and boarding Boyle, Murphy and Harry met in the lobby.

"Is your friend here?" Harry said.

"He'll be here any minute," Murphy said. "We'll meet him in the dining room."

Murphy and Harry were shown to a table in the hotel restaurant. A waiter brought them coffee. A few moments later, Judge Parker arrived.

"Hello, Murphy," Parker said.

"Judge, this is Harry Hastings," Murphy said. "Harry, this is Judge Isaac Parker."

"*The* Judge Parker?" Harry said, somewhat bedazzled.

102

Parker took a chair and looked at Murphy. "I can't tell you how distressed I was at the news of your father," Parker said. "I would have come to the funeral, but I was in the middle of a trial that couldn't be postponed."

"We got your telegram," Murphy said. "And that reminds me. I have to send one to Kai. I'll be right back."

After Murphy left the table, Harry said, "Forgive my curiosity, Judge, but what happened to Mr. Murphy's father?"

"He was murdered by two men a few weeks ago," Parker said. "And heaven help them when Murphy catches up to them."

"I thought Mr. Murphy was in the whiskey business," Harry said.

"Mr. Murphy is a US secret service agent, and the finest lawman I have ever known," Parker said. "His father and he partnered in making whiskey on the side. I can tell you this, if Murphy comes for you, there is no place to run and hide."

"That explains it," Harry said.

"What?" Parker said.

Harry told Parker about the incident in the saloon.

"Those men got off easy," Parker said. "Here he comes."

Murphy took his chair. "Sent a quick telegram to Kai," he said. "I feel like a steak."

After dinner, Murphy and Harry took drinks of bourbon to the porch. Murphy lit his pipe.

"Mr. Murphy, forgive me, but I asked the judge about your father," Harry said. "He told me he was murdered, and that you're a secret service agent and are after them men who murdered him."

"Harry, I should have told you about that," Murphy said. "Tomorrow, I want to make a proposition to you, but for tonight, I just want to enjoy the night air and my father's whiskey."

After breakfast, Harry made his rounds and Murphy went to the courthouse to see Judge Parker.

"I have a warrant from the Justice Department for the arrest of Moats and Holland," Murphy said. "Arthur would like them tried in your court."

Parker read the warrant. "Bring them to me, and they'll hang," Parker said. "Both of them."

"Holland has family in Oklahoma," Murphy said. "I'll be going there next."

"That little drummer, he told me about the incident in the saloon," Parker said. "He had no idea who you are."

"He's a good man," Murphy said. "I'll see you later, Judge."

Kai and the foreman took a buggy to town. The foreman drove. The first stop was at the freight company, where Kai made arrangements for one hundred barrels to be picked up and delivered to the railroad.

Then she went to the telegraph office and sent a wire to the bottling company to notify them one hundred barrels would be delivered in a week. While there, she picked up three telegrams from Murphy.

From the telegraph office, Kai went to the bank to make arrangements to have the money from the bottling company transferred to Mr. Murphy's account.

No one questioned Kai's authority to conduct business affairs for the Murphy family. No one wanted to deal with her husband's wrath if she were to be mistreated or looked down upon.

The last stop was the general store, where she loaded up on supplies.

Murphy waited for Harry on the porch of the hotel. He drank a cup of coffee and smoked his pipe. Around two in the afternoon, Harry appeared, carrying his sample case.

Murphy stood. "It's time to talk business, Harry," he said. "Come on, I rented a rig."

After picking up the rig, Murphy stopped by the general store, loaded up on supplies, and then headed for his house in the country.

"Where are we going?" Harry said.

"My home I told you about," Murphy said.

When they reached the house, Murphy's foreman was outside chopping wood.

"Mr. Murphy, I'm surprised to see you," the foreman said.

"How are things?" Murphy said.

"Very good," the foreman said. "I was terribly sorry to hear the news about your father. He was a true gentleman."

"Thanks," Murphy said. "And this little guy is Harry Hastings."

"Hello, Harry," the foreman said.

"Let's get the supplies in the house," Murphy said. "Harry, we'll stay the night."

Supper was fresh steaks from town, potatoes, carrots, and fresh bread. After supper, while the foreman tended to the horses, Murphy and Harry took coffee on the porch.

"Harry, let's talk," Murphy said. "Are you happy selling farm equipment?"

"Happy? I never thought about my work in that context," Harry said. "I suppose it's better than working in a store or a bank. The hours are long, but I'm mostly my own boss."

"Harry, I want you to come work for me," Murphy said.

"I'd be terrible in law enforcement," Harry said. "I've never even fired a gun."

Murphy smiled. "No, Harry, in the whiskey business," he said. "I believe my father makes the best bourbon anywhere, but outside of Tennessee and maybe Kentucky, most folks have never heard of it. I'd like you to represent us as our whiskey drummer. If you can sell plows, you can sell bourbon."

"Where?" Harry said.

"Everywhere. Anywhere. Back east, out west, north and south," Murphy said. "Your commissions will be excellent, and you can live wherever you wish when you're not working."

"You've given this some thought," Harry said.

"I have," Murphy said. "I've written a letter I want you to deliver to my wife. It explains everything."

Murphy reached into his jacket pocket for the letter and handed it to Harry. Harry read the letter and then looked at Murphy.

"There's a ten o'clock train to Tennessee tomorrow morning," Murphy said. "What do you say?"

"I guess I'd better not oversleep, or I'll miss the train," Harry said.

CHAPTER TWENTY-SEVEN

"You have the directions I wrote for you?" Murphy said.

"In my pocket," Harry said.

"And whatever you do, do not lose the letter to my wife," Murphy said.

"Also in my pocket," Harry said.

"Tell my wife and mother I'm headed to Oklahoma," Murphy said.

"I will," Harry said.

"Best get on the train before it leaves without you," Murphy said.

After Harry boarded the train, Murphy went to see Judge Parker.

"Little is known about those hills in the Ozarks, Murphy," Parker said. "Even the Indians from the reservation won't hunt there. If I knew an outlaw was hiding in those hills, I would send six or more marshals to do the job."

"It's best I go alone," Murphy said. "A large party only draws attention."

"When will you leave?"

"In the morning after I purchase supplies," Murphy said.

"Have dinner with me tonight," Parker said.

Late in the afternoon, Aideen sat on the porch with the baby. She noticed dust on the road in the distance. Someone was coming. The dust was too much for one rider and a horse. It was from a buggy.

Aideen waited until the buggy reached the gate and then she stood up. The buggy rode past the gate and stopped at the porch.

A little man in a blue suit stood up. "My name is Harry Hastings, and I am looking for the Murphy farm," he said.

"You found it," Aideen said.

"I have a letter from Mr. Murphy to Aideen and Kai Murphy," Harry said.

"Bring it to the porch," Aideen said.

Harry stepped down from the buggy and brought the letter to Aideen. She read it and handed it back to Harry. "Kai is down at the warehouse," she said. "Take your buggy and follow the road."

"Thank you," Harry said. He returned to the buggy and followed the road about a tenth of a mile to the large warehouse. Six wagons were being loaded with barrels of whiskey by burly men and Kai.

Kai wore pants, a sleeveless shirt, and gloves, and she rolled a barrel to a wagon. "That's one hundred," she said.

A man handed her a clipboard and pencil, and she signed her name to a document. Then she turned and looked at Harry.

"Who are you?" Kai said.

"I'd feel better if you let me send Reeves and Whitson with you," Parker said.

"That part of Oklahoma is out of your jurisdiction, Judge," Murphy said. "And besides, no sense in getting them killed along with me if the worst transpires."

They were having dinner in the hotel restaurant. Murphy had steak; Parker had chicken.

"Kai would be very upset with me if you got yourself killed," Parker said.

"I wouldn't be too happy about it myself," Murphy said. "That's why I'm expanding the whiskey business."

Parker looked at Murphy and then said, "The little farm-implement drummer, where is he?"

"About now he is with Kai and Aideen and about to become a whiskey drummer," Murphy said.

Parker shook his head. "Well, why the hell not?" he said. "A man should leave his wife well off."

"I thank you kindly for inviting me to dinner," Harry said.

"I've made up the spare bedroom for you to stay in until we get this figured out," Kai said. "Let's go to the den."

Kai, Aideen, and Harry went to Michael's den. A large map of the United States and its territories hung on the wall behind the desk.

"My husband suggested in his letter that you start with Missouri, Kansas, Colorado, and New Mexico," Kai said.

Harry looked at the map. "It's not too far off my farming route," he said. "Is there a print shop in town?"

"Yes," Kai said.

"I'll need to make some order pads to place orders with the bottling company," Harry said. "And I will need several sample cases."

"We'll go to town tomorrow morning," Kai said. "Let's take coffee on the porch."

A few minutes later, Kai, Aideen, and Harry sat in chairs drinking coffee on the porch and watched the setting sun.

"That story you told about the incident in the saloon, I'm surprised my husband didn't do far worse," Kai said.

"That's what Judge Parker said," Harry said.

"My son has been known to have serious lapses of ill temper," Aideen said.

Kai laughed. "That is putting it mildly," she said.

CHAPTER TWENTY-EIGHT

Murphy had breakfast with Judge Parker at the hotel before heading to the general store for supplies.

"If you don't get yourself killed, I would like these two men alive, if at all possible," Parker said. "It would be my profound pleasure to hang the both of them."

"I will do my best to satisfy your wish," Murphy said.

They parted with a handshake, then Murphy walked Boyle to the general store for supplies.

He purchased enough for ten days, loaded them onto the saddle, and rode west out of Fort Smith.

"I think ten order pads will do to start," Harry said.

"Make sure the address of the bottling company in Saint Louis is correct," Kai told the clerk.

"Yes, Mrs. Murphy," the clerk said.

"Harry, let's try the general stores for sample cases," Kai said.

"You want a drummer's case?" the clerk at the general store said. "For what goods?"

"Whiskey," Harry said.

"A whiskey case," the clerk said. "I got four that came from Saint Louis. Special ordered. Unfortunately the fellow was shot and killed in Wyoming before he got the chance to pick them up."

"Let's see them," Harry said.

The leather-bound cases held a dozen bottles of whiskey, with each bottle protected by a cushioned wall.

"We'll take them," Kai said. "Harry, let's go to lunch."

Murphy rode for five hours into the mountains of the Ozarks before stopping to give Boyle a rest and fix a hot lunch.

He built a fire and filled a pan with beans and bacon and put on the coffeepot, then tended to Boyle. While lunch cooked, Murphy gave Boyle a thorough brushing and a carrot stick as a reward. He didn't give Boyle any grain, as Boyle preferred grass for snacking.

Murphy poured a cup of coffee and sat with his back against the saddle. He sipped and grinned. "Come on out, Joseph, I made enough for two," he said loudly.

From behind a tree, Joseph Black Fox emerged and grinned at Murphy. "I just wanted to see if you slowed down any," he said.

"Not that much. Coffee?" Murphy said.

Joseph came to the fire, sat, and Murphy filled a second cup.

"Where's your hunting party?" Murphy said.

"A few miles to the east," Joseph said. "So who are you hunting this time?"

"Two men, murderers," Murphy said. "Have you seen two men recently? One on a brown bay with a white star on his nose, the other on a paint."

Joseph shook his head. "I'd remember," he said. "What makes you think they're here?"

"One of them has family on the Oklahoma side of the Ozarks," Murphy said.

"That's pretty bad country," Joseph said. "Even our hunting parties know better than to ride around in those hills."

"Want to share lunch?" Murphy said. "I made plenty."

"I could nosh," Joseph said.

"Nosh?" Murphy said.

"I heard the Indian agent say that once," Joseph said.

Murphy removed a second plate from a saddlebag and filled it with beans and bacon, then filled one for himself.

"I surly do love bacon," Joseph said. "These men, what do they look like?"

Murphy set his plate down, removed the two sketches from his pocket, and handed them to Joseph. "I haven't seen them. I'd remember," Joseph said and returned the sketches.

"How's the hunting?" Murphy said.

"Got two deer and an elk," Joseph said. "Who did those men murder?"

"My father," Murphy said.

"Shit."

"I got a special treat for you," Murphy said. "Pour us some more coffee."

Joseph filled the cups while Murphy removed a wrapped package from the supplies. "These are called graham crackers," he said.

"What are they?" Joseph said.

Murphy opened the wrapper and handed Joseph a cracker.

"What do you do with it?" Joseph said.

"You eat it," Murphy said.

Joseph bit into the cracker and looked at Murphy. "Pretty good," he said.

"I got two packages, why don't you take one," Murphy said.

"I will. Thanks," Joseph said. "Want me to ride with you?"

"No thanks, Joseph. If they see me they might shoot, but if they see you, they definitely will shoot," Murphy said. "No sense us both getting shot."

"Travel well, Murphy," Joseph said.

"And you," Murphy said.

Joseph mounted his horse. "Thanks for the crackers," he said.

Kai and Harry left the restaurant and walked to the telegraph office. A reply came from the bottling company. They would be happy to fill any and all orders sent to them from Harry Hastings, the telegram read.

Kai replied that Harry would begin work as soon as his order pads arrived.

"Let's get your cases and go home," Kai said. "We have much planning to do."

By nightfall, Murphy was in a part of the Ozarks he was totally unfamiliar with, in Oklahoma Territory.

He made camp, built a fire for supper, and then tended to Boyle.

"I don't know exactly where we are as yet," Murphy said as he brushed Boyle's thick back. "But no sense in looking unsavory."

CHAPTER TWENTY-NINE

After breakfast, Kai found Harry at the desk in Michael's den.

"Mrs. Murphy, please have a look," Harry said.

"Harry, please call me Kai," Kai said.

"All right, Kai," Harry said. "Please have a look and tell me what you think."

Kai stood next to Harry and looked at the sketchings he'd drawn on a pad. "What are these?" she said.

"Salesmanship," Harry said. "The labels on your whiskey are too plain. They don't jump out at you on the shelf. The farm equipment I sell is no different from anyone else's but what makes it sell is the packaging, the branding, and the showmanship. I can supply the showmanship, but the labels need much improvement."

"I think you are right, Harry," Kai said. "Which do you suggest?"

"The one here that says sipping whiskey," Harry said. "I think a golden drop pouring from the bottle with Murphy's Sipping Whiskey in bold lettering works best."

Kai studied the sketch.

"Done," she said. "We will contact the bottler tomorrow. Finish the sketch, and we will have samples made up at the print shop in town."

"Yes, ma'am," Harry said. "Kai, where do you think Murphy

is right now?"

"God only knows with that man," Kai said.

Murphy left camp at sunup, and by noon had traveled deep into the Oklahoma Ozarks. He wanted another hour in the saddle before breaking for lunch.

As he rode Boyle up a steep hill, a sharp pain struck Murphy in the side, followed by the crack of a rifle shot.

He fell from the saddle, rolled, and went still.

"Ya get him?" a man cried out.

"I got him," another voice said.

"Is he kilt?" a third voice said.

"He ain't moving," the second voice said. "I think he's kilt."

"Go check he's kilt. Go through his pockets and get all his shit," the first voice said. "That's a fine horse he's got."

As two men approached Murphy, he quietly removed his Colt from the holster and cocked it.

"Go through his pockets," a man said. "But I get his watch. I always wanted me a watch."

"What for? You can't tell time," the second man said.

"A man of stature always has himself a watch," the man said.

As one of the men knelt beside Murphy, Murphy rolled and shot the man in the face. The second man grabbed his pistol and Murphy shot him in the heart.

Murphy stood and looked at the third man, who was being stomped on by Boyle. Murphy walked to Boyle, took the reins, and calmed the massive horse down. The man's face was all but gone, thanks to Boyle's hooves.

Once Boyle was collected, Murphy checked his side. The bullet had creased a rib and probably, judging by the pain, cracked it.

"Well, this isn't helpful," Murphy told Boyle. "Not helpful at all."

Murphy tried to mount the saddle, but the sharp pain in his rib only grew worse.

"Stay put," Murphy said.

Murphy walked to a large clump of wild lettuce plants growing on the hill. He broke a stalk and watched the white liquid ooze out. The liquid was toxic; the leaves were not.

Murphy filled his hat with the leaves and returned to Boyle. "We need to distance ourselves from these bodies before nightfall when the wolves and coyotes come out to play," he said.

Murphy built a fire. Then he tore the leaves into tiny bits, put them into a cook pot, and added water. Once the water boiled, he let it simmer until all the water had evaporated, and all that was left was a thick sludge. He didn't have a strainer, so he used a spare neckerchief, poured the sludge onto the neckerchief, and wrapped it into a tight ball.

Then he squeezed the ball until all water was removed. What was left was a thick paste. Murphy took a small amount of the paste and ate it.

Then he sat against a tree and waited for the magic properties of the paste to kick in. It didn't take long for the pain in his side to subside.

He'd learned about wild lettuce from an army doctor during the war. The doctor had learned it from the Arapaho tribe he was visiting. The doctor called it opium lettuce.

Murphy removed the wood matches from his tinderbox and filled it with the paste. Then he poured whiskey over the cut in his side and mounted the saddle.

He rode until dark.

After supper, Kai, Aideen, and Harry took coffee to the porch. The night was warm, and the stars abundant in the sky.

"Mrs. Murphy . . . I mean Kai, where do you suppose Mr.

Murphy is right now?" Harry said.

"His last telegram said he was going into Oklahoma," Kai said.

"Do you think he's all right?" Harry said.

"My son has been shot seven times, stabbed at least four, and snake-bit twice, and he's still here," Aideen said. "If he is to be killed, it won't be by the likes of those two."

Kai sipped coffee and looked up at the stars.

"No sir, not by those two," she said.

Murphy looked up at the stars as he waited for the paste to kick in and ease the pain of his broken rib. As he waited, he stirred the pan of bacon and beans and sipped coffee to wash the taste of the paste from his mouth.

When the beans and bacon were cooked, he filled a plate, cut out a slice of cornbread, and ate with his back against the saddle.

Standing close by, Boyle was dozing.

Murphy looked at Boyle. "Tomorrow we need to make twenty miles," he said. "I know it's high country, but the map shows a settlement I'd like to reach before dark."

Boyle's response was to wiggle his ears.

"I can't say as I disagree with you," Murphy said.

A bit later, he took another pinch of the paste before settling in to sleep.

CHAPTER THIRTY

Kai and Harry showed the sketch of the label they wanted for the bottles to the printer at the print shop.

"How long will it take to print a dozen copies?" Kai said.

"Give me two days to set the block," the printer said.

"We'll be back in two days," Kai said.

From the print shop, Kai and Harry went to lunch at a restaurant in town. Harry had made a chart of his intended route after he had his order pads.

He unfolded the chart and showed it to Kai.

"Twenty cities and towns in two months is a lot of ground to cover," Kai said.

"It's how I've done it for years," Harry said. "After two months I take two weeks off and go home."

"Home to where?" Kai said.

"I don't know," Harry said. "I've always lived in hotels."

After breakfast, Murphy ate some of the paste. He was able to ride until midafternoon when he stopped to rest Boyle for an hour.

While Boyle munched on grass, Murphy took his binoculars with him and climbed a hill to a clearing. Using the binoculars, he was able to spot the settlement below in a clearing. The settlement consisted of several dozen tents, a few wood buildings, and one large corral.

Land had been cleared for farming. Some cattle grazed in a

field behind the farmland. Pigs were penned in at the edge of camp. Chickens pecked on the ground.

Murphy returned to Boyle and removed the saddle. "Your back will get a good rest," Murphy said. "We can't reach that settlement until dark, and I'd rather ride in when the sun is still up."

He built a fire and made a pot of coffee, then took a cup and the binoculars back up the hill. He took a closer look at the settlement below. There was a blacksmith working under a tent without sides. Near the corral, two men were shaving logs, readying them for building material.

A large tent housed a saloon. Another tent was being used as a cafeteria. A building was under construction that, when completed, would be a church.

They planned on the settlement being permanent.

Murphy returned to Boyle, gave him a good brushing, and fed him a bag of grain. Tomorrow's ride would be tasking, and Boyle needed the grain to sustain him.

Close to sunset, Murphy built up the fire and made a stew with meat from the general store in Fort Smith, potatoes, and beans. While the food cooked, he returned to the hill with the binoculars.

The day's work was done in the camp. Men were roasting a pig over a large fire. Women were setting tables. A man played a fiddle, and another man strummed a guitar.

This group seemed a tight-knit bunch and wouldn't give up information easily.

Murphy returned to Boyle and ate a hearty dinner with his back against the saddle. The rib didn't hurt as much, but he took a dose of the paste so he could get a good night's sleep.

Murphy had just coffee and two biscuits from the general store for breakfast. Then he saddled Boyle and started down to the settlement.

He reached the flats around noon. The settlement was a half mile or so away. As he neared the settlement, Murphy could see the inhabitants were getting ready for a group lunch.

As he rode closer, men started to line up with rifles, and women walked to the background.

When he reached the settlement, Murphy stared at thirty rifles aimed directly at him.

He stopped Boyle, looked at the thirty men aiming their rifles at him, and smiled. "Howdy," Murphy said.

An older man stepped forward. "State your business here," he said.

"I don't know as I have any," Murphy said.

"What's your name?" the older man said.

"What's yours?" Murphy said.

"Price."

"Murphy."

"State your business here, Murphy," Price said.

"Like I said, I don't know as I have any," Murphy said. "May I dismount without getting shot?"

"Go ahead, but remember these rifles," Price said.

Murphy dismounted and stretched his back.

"You got blood on your shirt there," Price said.

"Three men ambushed me a day and a half's ride from here," Murphy said. "I believe I have a cracked rib."

"What happened to the three men?" Price said.

"Worse," Murphy said.

"You still ain't said your business with us," Price said.

"I'm a lawman," Murphy said. "I have a warrant in my pocket for the arrest of two men. I'm going to reach for it and hand it to you."

"Go ahead," Price said.

Murphy reached for the warrant and handed it to Price, who read it quickly and handed it back to Murphy.

"Don't know them," Price said.

"Maybe some of your people do?" Murphy said.

"The womenfolk got lunch just about ready," Price said. "You're welcome to eat with us, and you can ask them then."

"Can I water my horse first?" Murphy said.

Price turned to the men behind him. "One of you men fetch water for his horse," he said. He turned to Murphy. "Sit at my table," he said.

The entire camp gathered at six large tables. The women served the noontime meal of fried chicken, potatoes, and carrots.

Then all heads bowed and Price said grace.

"Mr. Price, where are all you people from?" Murphy said.

"Alabama," Price said. "A few West Virginia transplants."

"Why here in the Ozarks?" Murphy said.

"One of our men came from here and stayed in Alabama after the war," Price said. "Most of us lost our farms and such and never recovered. I wanted to move west, and all these people here agreed to come with me. It took some time to raise the money and pool our assets, but we finally made it a year ago last month."

"You're building a town?" Murphy said.

"We are," Price said.

"How far to the nearest town if you need supplies?" Murphy said.

"Two days to the south on the flats," Price said. "We ain't had to go but a handful of times for nails and such. Our blacksmith makes our shoes and brackets and whatever else we need for building. We grow and raise most of what we eat, except for flour, sugar, and coffee."

"It looks to me like you'll have a fine town," Murphy said.

"We'll be no Montgomery, but that's what we came here to get away from," Price said.

"The man who led you here, may I speak to him?" Murphy said.

"Right after lunch," Price said.

Once the tables were cleared, Price walked Murphy to a house under construction where a woman in her thirties was washing clothes in a large basin.

"Where did Ben get to?" Price said.

"Went right to the fields," the woman said.

Price looked at Murphy. "Is that rib of yours up for a walk?"

"I'm fine," Murphy said.

The walk to the fields was about three hundred yards. A dozen men were working with hoes, turning the dirt.

"That fellow in the blue shirt is Ben Hogg," Price said. "Ben, come here a minute," Price shouted.

Hogg, a stout man of about forty, trotted over to Price and Murphy.

"Ben, Mr. Murphy wants a word with you," Price said.

"About what?" Hogg said.

"I'm looking for a family named Holland," Murphy said. "Maybe you know them, as you're from around here."

"I know them," Hogg said. "I can't say I'm the better for it."

"Where can I find them?" Murphy said.

"They had a farm twenty miles southwest of here," Hogg said. "I left to fight in the war when I was just seventeen, and I ain't been back since we settled here a year ago. I expect it's still there, though."

"How big a family?" Murphy said.

"There were three brothers, one sister, and their ma," Hogg said. "Their pa joined the war. I heard he was killed."

"Tom is the one I'm interested in," Murphy said.

"The middle brother," Hogg said. "Twenty years ago he was

bad. I expect he's worse now, if someone ain't killed him."

"Thanks for the information," Murphy said.

Hogg nodded and returned to the fields.

Price and Murphy returned to the camp.

"You'll stay the night," Price said. "We have six tubs, and I'll have the blood washed out of your shirt. I'll show you to a vacant tent, and our doc will look at your rib."

"You have a doctor?" Murphy said.

"From Montgomery," Price said. "Makes life a mite easier, having your own doctor."

As Murphy soaked in a hot tub, the doctor took a look at Murphy's rib.

"A bit to the right and you might not be here right now," the doctor said. "It's a clean wound, but I expect that rib smarts some."

"More than some," Murphy said.

"Yet you rode more than twenty miles to get here, I heard," the doctor said.

"I cooked a batch of wild lettuce to kill the pain," Murphy said.

"Army doctor?" the doctor said.

"During the war. He showed me how to cook a batch," Murphy said.

"Still need it?"

"I don't think so."

"If you have any left, keep it just in case," the doctor said. "Mind a personal question? What kind of lawman gets shot and stabbed so many times and comes back for more?"

"Secret service," Murphy said.

"I see," the doctor said. "Well, I will see you at dinner."

"Are you a married man, Mr. Murphy?" Price said.

"I am," Murphy said.

Dinner was steak with potatoes and carrots.

"Children?" Price said.

"A baby girl."

"It must be hard on them with you being away," Price said.

"It is, but my wife is a strong woman," Murphy said.

"This Holland and Moats. The warrant said they are wanted for murder," Price said. "In that context, they probably won't come peacefully."

"I'm kind of hoping not," Murphy said.

"Are you a drinking man, Mr. Murphy?" Price said.

"On occasion."

"Join me in my tent after dinner," Price said.

"The last trip to town, I had them pick this up for me," Price said. "I have yet to open it. I was saving it for when my house is complete, but that won't be until next spring I'm afraid."

Price opened a trunk and produced a bottle of brandy.

"Save that for your house," Murphy said. He removed the flask from his jacket pocket. "Got two glasses?"

Price fetched two glasses and Murphy added two ounces to each glass.

"To your house," Murphy said.

Price took a sip. "Very good stuff. What is it?"

"Bourbon whiskey."

"Next trip to town, I will remember it," Price said.

After bedding Boyle down for the night, Murphy was taken to a small tent with a cot and blankets and a chair. A hanging lantern burned on low flame.

Before turning in, he took the chair outside the tent, sat, and smoked his pipe. A hundred lantern lights illuminated tents and walking areas. Somebody played gentle guitar music. Soft laughter filled the gentle breeze.

The sky was clear, and stars twinkled by the thousands overhead.

It would be interesting to return in a few years and see what kind of a town these people built.

Cleveland was wrong. The west wasn't civilized and settled, as he claimed; it was just getting started.

CHAPTER THIRTY-ONE

After breakfast, Kai and Harry took the wagon to town to the print shop. The order pads and labels were ready.

From the print shop they went to the post office to mail the labels to the bottling company. Kai enclosed a note of instructions.

Kai suggested they go for coffee so they could discuss final details. They went to the café on Front Street and got a window table.

"What kind of deal did you have with the farm implement company in the way of expenses?" Kai asked.

"One thousand in expense money for eight weeks on the road," Harry said. "I was required to keep records and get receipts. My pay was ten percent of all business I drummed up."

"That sounds like a fair deal except let's up the percent to twelve," Kai said.

"That's very generous," Harry said.

"There is one more thing," Kai said. "On your off time, where will you live?"

"I still haven't given that much thought," Harry said.

"I have a suggestion," Kai said. "Murphy and I have our farm in Tennessee and our home in Fort Smith. We can't stay with Aideen forever. It would be nice if you stayed with her when you're not working. It would save you money and give her some company."

"Is that agreeable to her?" Harry said.

Kai nodded. "I already discussed it with her. It is."

"Then it's a deal," Harry said.

Murphy had breakfast at Price's table before leaving the settlement.

"How does that rib feel?" Price said. "The doc said it looks good."

"I expect it won't bother me much," Murphy said.

"I wish you'd give it a few more days to heal," Price said.

"I can't afford the time," Murphy said.

"No, I expect you'd like to catch up with those two," Price said. "But I hope you'll come back some day and see what we've built."

"I'd like that," Murphy said.

"You know, it occurs to me that we'll need a sheriff once we get things built," Price said. "Any advice on that?"

"Pick the most honest man you can find," Murphy said. "And next time you go to that town, send for some law books for guidance. He'll need them."

Price nodded. "Sound advice."

After breakfast, Price walked with Murphy to the corral where Boyle waited.

"I hope you don't mind. I had your saddlebags packed with fresh meat, coffee, and bread," Price said.

Murphy extended his right hand and shook with Price. "I don't mind," Murphy said.

The ride southwest was mostly on the flats. The grass was lush and green and the view of the surrounding mountains made for pleasant scenery.

Not even thirty years ago, this land belonged to the Indians. For centuries they had occupied the land. Life must have been good for them for a long time.

That way of life was gone. Too bad. Their way had been a good way, Murphy thought.

After fifteen miles or so, the terrain went from flat to hilly. He stopped to give Boyle a one-hour rest. Still full from breakfast, Murphy wasn't hungry, but he did make a half pot of coffee, drank two cups, and smoked his pipe while Boyle grazed on tall grass.

Over the next five miles, Murphy rode with caution. The hills came and went. Then he spotted smoke rising in the distance.

He stopped Boyle and dug his binoculars out of the saddle-bags. The smoke was rising from behind a hill. It rose and drifted on an easterly breeze.

"All right, boy, let's go for a look," Murphy said.

Murphy rode to the bottom of the hill the smoke rose above and dismounted. "Now you stay put," he told Boyle. Taking his Winchester and binoculars, he climbed to the top of the hill.

He got on his stomach and looked down. There was a farmhouse with a woman of about sixty sitting in a rocking chair. She was smoking a pipe and pulling on a jug. A shotgun rested against the wall to her right.

A woman around twenty-five was hanging laundry on a line between two trees.

On another line, a deer had been hung by its back legs to bleed out. Beside the house, a man chopped wood.

In a field to the right of the house, another man plowed behind a mule.

Murphy sighed, then returned to Boyle and mounted up. He rode Boyle to the top of the hill and then slowly down the other side to flat ground.

The woman on the porch spotted Murphy first. She stood and rang the dinner bell mounted on the cabin.

The woman hanging laundry turned and ran up to the porch.

The man chopping wood came running, ax in hand. The man plowing dropped the plow and ran to the house.

Murphy stopped thirty feet in front of the house, placing him outside of shotgun range.

The man with the ax and the man from the fields met in front of the porch.

"Get his horse, boys," the mother on the porch said. "We could use us a nice riding horse like that. He looks good for plowing, too."

The man with the ax charged Murphy. Murphy drew his Colt, shot the man in the shoulder, and he dropped to the ground.

"I'm shot," the man yelled. "I'm goddamn shot all to hell."

The other man raced to Murphy. "You shot my brother, you bastard sumbitch," he yelled.

Murphy waited until the man was close enough and then whacked him in the face with his Colt revolver.

The man fell to his knees, holding his broken nose. "Ya broke my nose, you bastard," he yelled.

The other man held his shoulder and cried, "I'm kilt for sure, you sumbitch."

Murphy slid down from the saddle. "You're not killed," he said.

The mother on the porch aimed the shotgun at Murphy. "I'll kill you where you stand," she said.

"From that distance I won't even feel it," Murphy said. He cocked the Colt and aimed it at the man with the broken nose. "Go ahead and shoot, and I'll do the same. If I'm not dead with your first shot, I'll kill your other boy."

"Now you just hold on, mister," the mother said. "We's just protecting what's ourn."

"Put that shotgun down and I'll ride on, and you can forget about the reward money," Murphy said.

"You hold on now. What reward money?" the mother said.

"You be kin to Tom Holland?" Murphy said.

"Who be asking?" the mother said.

"The law," Murphy said.

"Ma, I'm kilt," the man with the shoulder wound said.

"You broke my nose," the other man said.

"Shut up, the both of you," the mother said. She looked at Murphy. "Say what about a reward."

"Ten thousand dollars for information leading to the capture of John Moats and your son Tom," Murphy said.

"What'd they do?" the mother said.

"Robbery and murder," Murphy said.

"Ma, I'm bleeding to death here," the man with the wounded shoulder said.

"I told you to shut up," the mother said.

"Were they here or not?" Murphy said. "If not I'll move on."

"I'll say nothing until I see some righteous papers," the mother said.

Murphy reached into his pocket for the warrant. "I'll bring them to the porch," he said.

"Come ahead," the mother said. "June-Girl, go fix your brother's nose, and then take the bullet out of your other brother's arm."

"Yes, Ma," June-Girl said. She stepped down from the porch. "Let's go, you two. I ain't fixing you up out here."

Once the two men and June-Girl were inside the house, Murphy climbed the porch steps and stood over the woman.

"Can you read?" Murphy said.

The woman pulled a pair of spectacles out of her shirt pocket and slipped them on her nose. "Have a seat," she said.

Murphy took the chair next to her and handed her the warrant. She read it and lowered the paper.

"My son is fucked this time," she said.

"I would not have put it so vividly," Murphy said.

"But that's the gist of it," she said. "Ain't it?"

From inside the house, a man screamed.

"Now go clean out your nose and help me get this bullet out your brother's arm," June-Girl said.

"That's the gist of it," Murphy said.

"That reward be true?" the mother said.

"True enough," Murphy said.

"How much?"

"Ten thousand, but the information must be true and lead to their capture."

"You could have killed my boys had you wanted," the mother said. "Hell, you could have killed the lot of us if you wanted. Why didn't you?"

"Killing you wouldn't get me the information I came for," Murphy said.

From inside the house, a man screamed his head off. June-Girl said, "Hold still and be quiet, lest that bullet breaks up."

"Have you sipping whiskey to seal the deal?" the mother said.

Murphy took out his flask and opened the top. He took a sip and handed the flask to the mother. She took a sip and passed the flask back to Murphy.

"Jesus Christ! Mother of God," a man screamed from inside the house.

"The bullet's out, you big baby," June-Girl said.

The mother spat into her hand. Murphy spat into his hand, and they shook.

"Gimme another pull on that flask," the mother said.

Murphy handed her the flask.

"They was here all right," the mother said. "Tom and his friend. Tom said they was running from the law, but for what, he kept to himself. He's no good, that Tom. Always thieving and hurting folks. His pa was killed in the war when he was just

131

fifteen, so he had no male guidance. That's what done it. No male guidance."

The mother paused to take a sip of whiskey. "He said he was headed to Arizona to meet a friend in Tucson."

"Did he say who?" Murphy said.

"Not by name," the mother said.

"If this pans out, you've earned your reward," Murphy said.

"True enough?"

"True enough," Murphy said.

The mother passed the flask back to Murphy.

"Which way did they ride when they left?" Murphy said.

"South," the mother said. "Probably to the McAllister Settlement to catch the railroad about thirty miles from here."

Murphy removed one hundred dollars from his wallet and handed it to the mother. "Obliged," he said.

Murphy stood, walked down to Boyle, and mounted the saddle.

CHAPTER THIRTY-TWO

Kai served dinner in the small dining room off the kitchen. At the table sat Aideen and Harry.

"I've finalized the route for the first eight weeks," Harry said. "I'd like to leave the day after tomorrow, with the first stop in Saint Louis, then Columbus and Kansas City."

"I have something I want to show you after dinner," Kai said.

"I'll tend to the dishes," Aideen said. "You two finish your business."

"Come, Harry," Kai said.

Harry followed Kai to Michael's den.

"Take off your jacket," Kai said.

Kai opened the desk drawer and removed a .32 caliber revolver housed in a shoulder holster.

"I've never fired a gun," Harry said.

"And I pray you never do," Kai said. "But it's better to have it and not need it than to need it and not have it. Now you wear it on your left side."

Harry put the holster on and looked at Kai.

"It belonged to Murphy's father," Kai said.

"I can't take—" Harry said.

"It was Aideen's idea," Kai said. "You wouldn't want to insult your host, would you?"

"No, I wouldn't," Harry said.

"Now let's have coffee on the porch and watch the stars," Kai said.

Murphy rode fifteen miles before sunset and then made camp. He built a fire and put on a pot of coffee, then checked his supplies. His saddlebags were full of fresh beef, pork, beans, sugar, and a tin with eight brown eggs in it.

He settled on the beef, with beans, and then tended to Boyle. He gave the horse a thorough brushing, then gave him a bag of grain.

As he ate, Murphy checked what maps he had of the territory. The McAllister Settlement was a railroad stop erected a few years ago as a place for the railroad to do repairs and service cars.

Otherwise it wouldn't exist. But because it did exist and was a railroad repair yard, they would have a telegraph.

With an early start, he could be there by noon.

After eating, Murphy lit his pipe, splashed a bit of bourbon in a cup, and watched the stars and thought about Kai, his mother, and the baby.

A mile from the settlement were several sets of railroad tracks with cars lined up for a hundred yards. Some men worked on repairs, while others tested engines. Thick plumes of black smoke from the engines filled the air.

Murphy rode past the men and reached the chaotic, muddy streets of the McAllister Settlement.

Some buildings were constructed of wood, primarily the saloons, a hotel, and a few shops. Others were constructed partially using wood and canvas. Some were just tents and lean-tos.

One saloon was two stories with a balcony. A dozen whores stood on the balcony and watched the streets. Two men were fighting in the mud, and nobody seemed to pay them any mind.

One man grabbed a piece of firewood off the wood sidewalk and bashed the other man's head open with it. "There, ya sumbitch," the man with the firewood said. "That will teach ya."

The other man, blood streaming down his face, pulled a gun and shot the first man. Then both men fell dead in the mud. The event went seemingly unnoticed by people in the streets.

Murphy rode around them and stopped at a wood building marked Railroad Police. He dismounted and tied Boyle to the hitching post.

"Any man comes near, you stomp him good," Murphy said.

Murphy entered the railroad police office. A large man wearing a blue uniform sat behind a desk. He looked at Murphy.

"Help you?" he said.

"You got two dead men out there in the mud," Murphy said.

"Somebody will pick them up a'for long."

"What's your name?" Murphy said.

"Who's asking?"

Murphy tossed his wallet on the desk. The large man opened it and looked at Murphy's identification. "Secret service, huh," he said.

Murphy took his wallet back and said, "And you are?"

"Name is James Pitt. I'm chief of railroad police in McAllister Settlement."

"Well, Pitt, I didn't just happen by," Murphy said. "I'm here in—"

"Hold on," Pitt said. "Tell me your troubles over a drink." He stood up. "Follow me," he said.

Murphy followed Pitt outside to the wood sidewalk. Two sanitation workers were picking up the dead bodies from the mud and tossing them into wheelbarrows.

"Across the street there," Pitt said.

Murphy took Boyle's reins and walked across the muddy

street to the Oasis Saloon.

After tying Boyle to the hitching post, Murphy followed Pitt into the saloon to the bar. The bartender was bandaging the left arm of a woman dressed in a sheer robe.

"What happened here, Jewel?" Pitt said.

"That bastard Cos stabbed me," Jewel said.

Pitt turned and looked at a skinny fellow at a table, drinking a beer. "Is that right, Cos? Did you stab Jewel?" he said.

"She didn't service me right," Cos said.

"It ain't my fault you can't last," Jewel said.

"Well, you tease a man too much," Cos said.

"Jewel, did he pay you?" Pitt said.

"No, he did not," Jewel said.

"Pay her, Cos," Pitt said.

Cos stood up and put a five-dollar-gold piece on the bar.

"Make it ten," Pitt said.

"Ten?" Cos said.

"For the stabbing," Pitt said. "You just can't stab a girl without compensation."

Cos put another five-dollar piece on the bar. "I'll never come back here," he said.

"You'll be back," Jewel said as Cos walked out. "Next time your bean needs wiggling."

Pitt looked at the bartender. "Fred, two whiskeys, if you please."

The bartender set up two shot glasses and Pitt carried them to a table. Murphy joined him.

"Now then, what can I do for you?" Pitt said.

"I have a warrant for two men," Murphy said. "I believe they came here to take the railroad."

"What did they do?" Pitt said.

"Murder."

"In case you haven't noticed, this place isn't exactly the most law-abiding settlement on the map," Pitt said. "Half the people in town can lay claim to such a charge."

Murphy took out the sketches of Moats and Holland and showed them to Pitt.

"Wasting your time with me," Pitt said. "The whores are the ones would have seen them."

"How many whores are there?" Murphy said.

"A dozen ladies."

"Any other place have ladies?" Murphy said.

"This is the only stop in town."

"Get them all down here," Murphy said.

Pitt looked at Murphy.

"I wasn't asking," Murphy said.

"Jewel, get all the girls down here," Pitt said.

Before Jewel could move, Cos rushed back in. "I changed my mind. I'd like another turn," he said.

Murphy stood up, grabbed Cos by the back of his shirt and belt, and threw him out the swinging door. "The bar is closed until I say it's open," Murphy said. "Jewel, get all the ladies down here."

Jewel stared at Murphy.

"Go," Murphy said.

Jewel turned and ran up the stairs to the second floor. Murphy returned to Pitt, picked up his drink, and downed the shot.

"That hotel across the street any good?" Murphy said.

"Nope," Pitt said.

"The food any good?" Murphy said.

"Nope," Pitt said.

Jewel led eleven other women down the stairs to the bar.

"Ladies, have a seat," Murphy said. "Any that wants a drink, it's on me."

The women sat at two tables. The bartender set up a dozen

shots of whiskey and brought them to the tables.

"My name is Murphy, and I am a US secret service agent," Murphy said. "I have a warrant for two men I am trailing. I'd like to show you a sketch of them and have you identify them, if possible."

"What's a secret man servant do?" one of the women said.

"Secret service agent, Liz," Pitt said. "He's a federal lawman."

"How I'm supposed to know what he is?" Liz said.

"I'm after two men wanted for murder," Murphy said. "I believe they came through here about two weeks ago. I figure you ladies might remember them."

Murphy handed the two sketches to Jewel. She shook her head no and passed the sketches to the other girls.

"I know him," one of the girls said. "I remember 'cause he had a belly scar."

Murphy looked at the sketch of Moats. "Are you sure?" he said.

The girl nodded. "I'm sure. He wanted to spank me over his knee and have me call him Daddy."

All the ladies laughed at that. Murphy raised his hand to quiet them. "The other one?" Murphy said.

"I had him," Liz said. "I recognize his face. He was a talker, that one. Said they was going to New Mexico. No, Arizona."

Murphy removed one hundred and twenty dollars from his wallet and gave it to Jewel. "You divide this up among the ladies," he said.

Murphy retrieved the two sketches and nodded to the ladies. Then he and Pitt walked out of the saloon. Standing on the wood sidewalk was Cos, who glared up at Murphy.

"No man throws me on the street," Cos said.

Murphy grabbed Cos by the shirt and threw him back into the saloon.

"Where's the railroad station?" Murphy said.

"The whole damn town is the station," Pitt said.

"Where you can buy a ticket?" Murphy said.

"Oh. At the edge of town, past Oak Street," Pitt said.

Murphy untied Boyle and said, "Lead the way."

Seven blocks later, they arrived at the railroad station. Murphy tied Boyle to a post, then he and Pitt entered.

A clerk was behind the counter, reading a newspaper.

"Afternoon, Pitt," the clerk said.

"This is Murphy," Pitt said. "He's a federal agent tracking two murderers."

Murphy slid the sketches across the counter to the clerk. The clerk studied them for a few seconds. "I remember them," he said. "They paid for passage for their horses. One of the horses was a paint."

"To where?" Murphy said.

"Let me think," the clerk said. "Arizona. No, New Mexico. No, Arizona. Tucson, I believe."

"When is the next train to Tucson?" Murphy said.

"Day after tomorrow at noon," the clerk said. "If it's on time."

"Marvelous," Murphy said.

"Want to check into the hotel?" Pitt said.

"Yeah," Murphy said. "And send a telegram."

The hotel had decent accommodations. Upon checking in, Murphy ordered a bath. The tub was a bit small, but he made do. Afterward, he sent his dirty clothes to the hotel laundry.

Leaving the hotel, Murphy found the telegraph office a few fronts down from Pitt's office. He went in and sent a telegram to Kai. On the way out, he met Pitt on the street.

"It's been a good day so far," Pitt said. "Only two people killed and the one stabbing."

"That hotel serve a good steak?" Murphy said.

"More or less," Pitt said. "More less, but it's edible."

"Let's go," Murphy said.

The steak was surprisingly not as bad as Murphy thought it would be. It came with potatoes, carrots, beans, and rolls.

"How long have you been with the railroad?" Murphy said.

"Since sixty-seven," Pitt said.

"I've been in some railroad camps, but this one beats them all," Murphy said.

"It's supposed to be temporary. Least that's what I was told back in eighty-one," Pitt said. "But as a repair yard it serves a purpose, so I guess it will be here a while longer."

"I worked railroad police back in sixty-seven through seventy-one at Grant's request," Murphy said.

"I was southern, but our paths may have crossed before," Pitt said. "You work the joining of the two railroads?"

"I did."

"I would have liked to see that," Pitt said. "How about a drink? I got a fresh bottle in my desk."

"A drink usually settles the stomach after a steak," Murphy said.

"Let's go," Pitt said.

They crossed the street and entered Pitt's office. Pitt removed a sealed bottle of whiskey and two glasses from his desk. He used a pocketknife to crack the seal on the bottle, and then poured two ounces into each glass.

"Here's how," Pitt said.

"Here's how," Murphy said.

Each man took a sip.

From outside, a man screamed, "This time I'll do it. I mean it. I'll do it."

"Now what?" Pitt said.

Pitt and Murphy left the office. Across the street, on the

balcony of the saloon, Cos held a knife to Jewel's throat.

"I'll cut her ear to ear, this bitch," Cos screamed. "I swear I will."

A large crowd had gathered in the muddy street. Fred, the bartender, was in the crowd.

"Leave her be, Cos," Fred said. "She did you no harm."

"She won't laugh at me no more," Cos said. "It ain't my fault I got a hair trigger. She could be nurturing. She ain't got to laugh at me. Well, she won't laugh at me no more."

Murphy and Pitt walked to the center of the street.

"Put that knife down, Cos," Pitt said. "You're not cutting anybody."

Cos pressed the tip of the blade against the side of Jewel's throat and a drop of blood appeared.

Jewel cried out.

Murphy drew his Colt and kept it by his side. "I'm counting to three," he said. "If that knife isn't on the deck by three, I'm going to kill you."

"Screw you," Cos said.

"One," Murphy said, and the crowd began to buzz.

Cos ripped open Jewel's blouse, exposing her breasts.

"Two," Murphy said and cocked the Colt.

"Screw all of you!" Cos hollered.

Murphy raised the Colt and fired. The left side of Cos's neck exploded, and he fell dead to the floor of the deck.

Jewel screamed and ran inside.

Pitt looked at Murphy as Murphy slowly replaced the Colt to the holster.

"Somebody get the doctor to have a look at that asshole," Pitt said.

Murphy sighed. "Let's finish our drink," he said.

Murphy removed his boots, sat in the chair, and lit his pipe. He felt weary and drained and—dare he think it? Old.

There was a soft knock on the door and he stood and went to answer it. Wearing a clean dress, her hair freshly washed, Jewel smiled at him.

"Jewel, what are you doing here?" Murphy said.

"Fred sent me over to say thanks for saving my life," Jewel said.

"You're welcome," Murphy said.

"Can I come in?" Jewel said. "Fred said I should give you a free one, for saving my life the way you did."

"Come in," Murphy said.

Jewel entered the room and Murphy closed the door. He looked at her neck. "It's not too bad," he said.

"Thanks to you," Jewel said.

"I was just about to have a drink," Murphy said. He dug one of his flasks out of a saddlebag and poured an ounce into two glasses and gave one to Jewel.

Jewel tossed back the whiskey and set the glass on the table. "Well, let's get to it," she said and started to unbutton her blouse.

"Now just hold it," Murphy said.

"Is something wrong?" Jewel said. "The doc checks me every week. I'm clean. Honest I am."

"I'm a married man," Murphy said.

"So are most of the men who come see us," Jewel said. "And being married never stopped a man from his pleasures."

"And I love my wife," Murphy said.

"I don't understand," Jewel said.

"Sleep on it. It will come to you," Murphy said.

Jewel looked up at Murphy, nodded, and then left the room.

Murphy slowly sat in his chair. "Marvelous," he said and tossed back his drink.

CHAPTER THIRTY-THREE

Pitt joined Murphy in the restaurant for breakfast.

"The whole camp is buzzing about the shooting last night," Pitt said.

"I think I might take a ride this morning," Murphy said. "My horse gets restless if he doesn't get to run every few days."

"I have to ride out to the repair yard to check a few things. Why not ride along with me?" Pitt said.

"All right," Murphy said. "I'll get my horse and meet you at your office."

After breakfast, Murphy walked to the livery to get Boyle. As he passed the saloon, Jewel came out and said, "Mr. Murphy."

"Good morning, Jewel," Murphy said.

"I slept on it," Jewel said. "I think what you meant is that you want to stay true to your wife because you love her. Is that right?"

"That's right," Murphy said. "And because if she found out, she'd shoot me dead on the spot."

Jewel grinned.

"She would, too," Murphy said.

After retrieving Boyle from the livery, Murphy rode to Pitt's office where Pitt was mounted and waiting.

They followed the repair tracks out of camp for about a mile to where workers were repairing cars and engines.

"How's it going, men?" Pitt said. "Any theft last night?"

"Not much," a worker said. "Them dogs you got us is sav-

143

ages. They'd tear a man apart as soon as sniff them."

"When's the supply train due in?" Pitt said.

"About an hour," the worker said. "If it's on time."

"Murphy, I have to stay and take inventory," Pitt said. "I'll see you later."

Murphy nodded and rode in a southeast direction onto the prairie. Boyle was full of pent-up energy and wanted to run. Murphy let him go for about five miles. Then he slowed Boyle to a stop beside a creek and dismounted.

Murphy removed the saddle and brushed Boyle's coat. "You can drink when you've cooled off and not before," Murphy said.

Once Boyle was brushed and cool, Murphy sat against a tree and smoked his pipe. Boyle found a sweet patch of grass to munch on before taking a drink from the creek.

"Ready to head back?" Murphy said when his pipe was spent.

After saddling Boyle, Murphy started back at a leisurely pace. That's when he noticed wagon tracks in the grass.

"Hold on," he said. He dismounted, knelt, and inspected the tracks. The impressions were deep. The wagon was heavy. The tracks came directly from the railroad repair yard and they were fresh, no more than ten or twelve hours old.

He mounted the saddle and rode back to the camp.

Pitt was at his desk, doing paperwork, when Murphy walked in.

"How's your inventory?" Murphy said.

"Having a difficult time accounting for certain items," Pitt said. "Not in delivery, but in usage."

"I think I know why," Murphy said.

"Why?" Pitt said.

"Get your horse," Murphy said.

Murphy and Pitt inspected the wagon tracks left in the prairie.

"The wagon was heavy," Pitt said.

"Maybe with railroad supplies," Murphy said.

"I wouldn't have thought it possible anybody could get past those dogs," Pitt said.

"Unless the men taking care of the dogs are the men doing the stealing," Murphy said.

"Son of a bitch," Pitt said.

"You got a new shipment today," Murphy said.

"I did, yes," Pitt said.

"Feel up to a night ride?" Murphy said.

"We've been out here two hours now," Pitt said.

"Go back if you want to," Murphy said. "I'll stay."

"That's not what I meant," Pitt said.

Murphy and Pitt were seated against a tree with a view of the prairie. The moon was close to full, and bright, and they could see well enough.

"Listen," Murphy said.

"What is that?" Pitt said.

"Singing."

Murphy and Pitt walked to the old tracks. They saw a wagon riding toward them. Two men were singing.

Once a jolly swagman camped by a billabong, Under the shade of a coolabah tree. And he sang as he watched and waited till his "Billy" boiled. You'll come a-waltzing Matilda, with me.

"You got to be kidding me," Pitt said.

"They're drunk," Murphy said.

"An understatement," Pitt said.

"What do we do now?"

"Wait. They'll be here soon enough.

145

Waltzing Matilda, Waltzing Matilda, you'll come a-waltzing, with me.

"They sound like somebody bit the head of a chicken," Pitt said.

"Get the lanterns," Murphy said.

Pitt walked back to the horses and returned with two large oil lanterns.

"Light them with the flame on high and set them down in their path," Murphy said.

Pitt lit the lanterns and set them on the ground.

"Now step back about ten feet. They won't be able to see in the light," Murphy said.

Murphy and Pitt moved back about ten feet and waited.

"Gimme a pull on the jug," a voice said.

"Hey, what's them lights there?" a second voice said.

"What lights?" the first voice said.

"Them lights there right in front of us," the second voice said.

"Stop the wagon and let's see," the first voice said.

The wagon stopped in front of the two lanterns.

"Some shitbird is out there," the first voice said.

"Well, I didn't think no cow lit them lanterns," the second voice said.

In the dark, Murphy cocked his Colt, "That sound you heard is me cocking my Colt, which is aimed right at your heads," Murphy said.

"I told you some shitbird was out there," the first voice said.

Murphy nodded to Pitt, and they came upon the wagon from its flank. When they were close enough, Pitt said, "Charlie, what are you doing stealing railroad property?"

"This fellow paid us to deliver these items to him," the first voice said.

"What fellow?" Murphy said.

146

"Down the road a piece," the first voice said. "Said he needs this stuff for the Southern Pacific."

"How far down the road?" Murphy said.

"Another maybe three, four miles," the second voice said.

Murphy looked at Pitt. "You game?"

"Just the two of us?" Pitt said.

"You two get out of the wagon," Murphy said.

The two men climbed down.

"Now start walking back to the camp," Murphy said.

"Can we take the jug?" the first voice said.

"Yeah, you can take the jug," Murphy said. "And for God's sake, don't sing until we're out of range."

Murphy smoked his pipe as Pitt drove the wagon.

"Maybe this isn't such a good idea," Pitt said.

"I can take it in alone," Murphy said.

"I didn't say I was abandoning you. I said maybe it wasn't such a good idea," Pitt said.

"I see a fire," Murphy said.

"Yeah, I see it too," Pitt said.

"We'll wait for us to get closer," Murphy said.

"For what?"

"Me to get out," Murphy said.

"Out?" Pitt said.

"Another hundred yards," Murphy said. "And when I get out, sing."

"Sing?"

"Not until I get out," Murphy said.

Five or so minutes later, Murphy hopped off the wagon. "Start singing," he said.

"Waltzing Matilda, Waltzing Matilda, you'll come a-waltzing with me," Pitt sang.

Murphy ran through the darkness and came up behind two

large wagons where three men stood watch beside a fire.

Murphy came up behind the three men and waited for Pitt to arrive in the wagon.

"Drunken fools," one of the men said.

"As long as they bring us what we need," another man said.

Finally Pitt arrived in the wagon.

"Why that ain't them. That's Pitt," the first man said.

"Well, shit, we'll have to kill the sumbitch," the second man said.

From behind the three men, Murphy said, "I wouldn't do that if I was you."

In the wagon, Pitt pulled his pistol and aimed it at the three men.

"Front or back, it's up to you," Murphy said.

"Well, shit," the second man said.

"Toss your weapons, and put your hands up," Murphy said.

The three men didn't move.

"I wasn't asking," Murphy said.

Most of the residents of the camp lined the streets to watch Murphy on Boyle lead the wagon full of prisoners to Pitt's office.

From the balcony of the saloon, Jewel and the other women watched as Murphy dismounted and stood on the sidewalk as Pitt filed the five prisoners into the office.

"Well, Pitt, I have just enough time for breakfast and a hot bath before my train arrives," Murphy said.

After having breakfast with Pitt, Murphy stepped out to the wood sidewalk with Pitt. There they saw two men fighting in the muddy street.

"Ya sumbitch, I'll kill you," one of the men said.

"Not if I kill you first," the second man said.

"Ever hear of Grover Cleveland?" Murphy said.

"No, sir. Who is he?" Pitt said.

"Just a man who said the west was civilized," Murphy said.

"He sounds dumb enough to run for president," Pitt said.

CHAPTER THIRTY-FOUR

At the train station, Kai and Aideen hugged Harry.

"Be safe," Kai said. "And telegraph often."

"I'll be back in eight weeks," Harry said.

After Harry boarded the train, Kai and Aideen returned to the buggy where the baby slept in her carrier.

"Let's go to lunch," Kai said.

They went to the café near the print shop. Kai set the baby's carrier beside her at the table.

"I had a dream last night that all of this was a dream, and that Michael was alive and well," Aideen said. "Then I woke up. And the dream faded."

The baby woke up and Kai lifted her from the carrier.

"When my son comes home, don't ever let him go out again," Aideen said. "Break his legs if you have to, but you keep him home."

The moment Murphy's head hit the pillow in his sleeping car, he was sound asleep. He didn't move for seven hours and awoke in time for dinner.

After washing up in the basin in his room, Murphy changed his shirt and went to the dining car. There was just one small vacant table beside a window, so he took it. The waiter came to the table and Murphy ordered a steak and a cup of coffee.

The coffee arrived first. Murphy sipped and looked out the window.

A shadow fell across the table and a male voice said, "Excuse me old-timer, but this seat appears to be the only one available. Might I join you at your table?"

Murphy looked at the young man of about twenty who stood over the table. He was above average height, slim, sandy-haired, and had blue eyes. He was dressed as a cowboy, although the clothes were new, and he wore a pearl-handled Colt revolver in a brown holster on the right side of his hips.

"Have a seat," Murphy said.

"Thanks, old-timer," the young man said. He took the chair and said, "They call me the Oklahoma Kid."

"Really," Murphy said.

"True enough. What do they call you?"

"Murphy."

"Pleased to know you, Murphy."

The waiter came to the table and the Kid ordered a steak.

"Where you headed?" Murphy said.

"Denver, to make my fortune," the Kid said. "I'm gonna be famous."

"Really?" Murphy said.

"True enough," the Kid said.

"Famous for what?" Murphy said.

"My prowess with a firearm," the Kid said. "But I don't expect an old-timer like you to know of such things."

"So you're fast with that thing?" Murphy said.

"I would demonstrate, but we're in mixed company and it wouldn't be polite," the Kid said.

"I understand," Murphy said.

The waiter brought the steaks to the table.

"So where are you headed?" the Kid said.

"Tucson."

"I thought about Tucson, but I read it's really dry," the Kid said. "I like a wetter climate myself."

151

"Denver certainly is that," Murphy said.

"You've been there?"

"Many times."

"What line are you in, Murphy?"

"Whiskey."

"You a drummer?" the Kid said.

"You might say."

"That's too dull of a life for me," the Kid said. "No offense, but I seek fame and fortune. I am to get both or die trying."

"By using that gun?" Murphy said.

"It's as good a way as any and better than most," the Kid said.

"And getting killed doesn't bother you?" Murphy said.

"Getting killed isn't in my plan," the Kid said.

"How about a drink after dinner, Kid?" Murphy said.

"A drink would be nice," the Kid said.

They went to the gentlemen's car. Murphy got a bottle of bourbon and two glasses, and he and the Kid took a table by a window.

Murphy opened the bottle and filled both glasses to the brim.

"Well, Kid, a toast to your success," Murphy said. He downed half the glass in two quick swallows.

"Thank you kindly," the Kid said and took a quick gulp.

Murphy downed his drink and said, "Drink up, Kid. The night is young."

The Kid gulped his drink and set the glass on the table. Murphy refilled both.

"Come on, Kid. The night is young, and we have some drinking to do," Murphy said and drank half his glass.

The Kid took several gulps of his drink and his eyes started to water.

"All the way, Kid," Murphy said.

By the time Murphy refilled the glasses the fourth time, the

Kid said, "No more for me please. I've had enough."

"I'll let you know when you've had enough, Kid," Murphy said. "You wouldn't want to insult me, would you?"

The Kid took two more sips and then said, "I don't feel so good, Murphy."

"This way, Kid," Murphy said.

Murphy took him between cars where the Kid leaned over the platform and vomited for a solid ten minutes. Finally, the Kid stood up and looked at Murphy.

"Everything is spinnin' round and round," the Kid said.

"Which is your sleeping car, Kid?" Murphy said.

"Nine."

Murphy tossed the Kid over his shoulder, slid open the door, and carried him to the sleeper cars to number nine. By the time Murphy set the Kid down on the bed, he was passed out cold.

"You'll have a headache come morning, Kid, and hopefully will have learned some humility along the way," Murphy said.

CHAPTER THIRTY-FIVE

After a somewhat refreshing night's sleep, Murphy walked Boyle along the platform at the railroad station in Tucson, Arizona.

First established as a mail delivery route from Texas to California, Tucson was home to eight thousand residents who mostly catered to the many surrounding cattle ranchers. It was also where Frank Stilwell had attempted to assassinate Wyatt Earp the night he took his brother Virgil to the Tucson railroad station in eighty-two.

As Murphy walked through the dusty streets, the temperature was around ninety degrees and the air dry as dust.

The Hotel Tucson was the largest in town and had its own livery. After checking into the hotel, Murphy brought Boyle to the livery. "Give him plenty of hay and grain, and pick up four new shoes when you get a chance," he told the livery manager.

"Want me to have the blacksmith shoe him?" the manager said.

"I'll do that myself," Murphy said. "He won't allow anybody else to do it."

From the livery, Murphy walked along wood sidewalks to the sheriff's office. At least half the population was Mexican in origin.

When he reached the sheriff's office, Murphy opened the door and stepped inside. Two deputies and the sheriff, who was at his desk, were drinking coffee.

They looked at Murphy.

"Carl?" Murphy said.

Sheriff Carl Woodward stood up from behind the desk and walked to Murphy. "What the hell are you doing here, Murphy?" Woodward said.

"I heard you moved south when you retired," Murphy said. "Why here?"

"My wife is from here," Woodward said. "Boys, this here is Murphy. We served together in the secret service."

Murphy nodded to the two deputies.

"So what brings you to Tucson?" Woodward said.

"Had breakfast?" Murphy said.

"I was just about to do that," Woodward said. "Boys, the town is yours until I return."

Woodward led Murphy six blocks down a side street to a moderately sized, Spanish-style home.

"Your place?" Murphy said.

"Come in and meet the missus," Woodward said.

The interior of the house was a mixture of Spanish and American decor.

"Pilar, where are you?" Woodward shouted.

"Kitchen," Pilar said.

"Come out here for a minute," Woodward said.

Pilar, a beautiful Mexican woman of about forty, dressed in a robe, entered the living room. She looked at Murphy and immediately started yelling at Woodward in Spanish.

"English, honey. Please," Woodward said.

"Why you no tell me you bring company?" Pilar said with a heavy Spanish accent. "I no dressed for company."

"Murphy just arrived and . . . okay, go change," Woodward said. "We'll have coffee in the kitchen."

"Stir the bacon," Pilar said.

Woodward and Murphy went to the kitchen. A pot of coffee rested on the stove, as did a pan of bacon. Woodward filled two cups, stirred the bacon, and then he and Murphy sat at the table.

"You're not here on assignment, and you're not here on vacation, because God knows why would you be?" Woodward said. "So what brought you to Tucson?"

"A warrant," Murphy said.

"Since when does the secret service serve warrants?" Woodward said.

"Since the men I'm serving it on robbed and murdered my father," Murphy said.

"I see," Woodward said.

Pilar, clad in a sleeveless dress, entered the kitchen. "I told you stir the bacon," she said.

"I did," Woodward said.

"Go outside with your coffee," Pilar said. "You're useless in a kitchen."

"Yes, ma'am," Woodward said.

Woodward took Murphy through an open door to the backyard, where a table and chairs were shaded by an awning.

They set their coffee cups on the table and took chairs.

"These men, you think they're in Tucson?" Woodward said.

"Or were," Murphy said.

Pilar appeared with a large platter loaded with tortillas, scrambled eggs, bacon, and potatoes.

"I get you more coffee," Pilar said.

"Then sit and have breakfast with us," Woodward said.

Pilar nodded and went inside.

"Where are your boys?" Murphy said.

"School," Woodward said. "They'll be home after three."

Pilar returned with the coffeepot and took the chair between Woodward and Murphy. "I remember you from Washington," Pilar said. "We met a few times at the formal affairs."

"I remember," Murphy said.

"Eat," Pilar said. "Before it gets cold."

Murphy spooned scrambled eggs into a tortilla, rolled it, added bacon and potatoes to his plate, and took a bite.

"Very good," Murphy said.

"You are married now?" Pilar said. "You had no wife in Washington."

"I am," Murphy said.

"No kidding. You?" Woodward said.

"No kidding, and we have a baby daughter," Murphy said.

"That's wonderful," Woodward said.

"What is your wife's name?" Pilar said.

"Kai."

Pilar looked at Murphy. "Sioux or Navajo?" she said.

"A bit of both, with Irish and German for good measure," Murphy said.

"My ancestors were Mexican Comanche," Pilar said.

"I have to get to work, honey," Woodward said.

Pilar looked at Murphy. "You come for dinner?"

"Of course, he will," Woodward said.

Woodward looked at the two sketches, then showed them to two of his deputies. "I don't recall them, but we got eight thousand residents here now," he said.

"If they was just passing through and had some money to burn, they'd probably stop at the Palace Saloon," a deputy said. "That's where the sporting ladies are."

"He's right," Woodward said.

"I've been down this road before," Murphy said. "Let's go."

Woodward looked at his deputies. "One word gets back to Pilar, and I'll skin you both alive," he said.

The Palace Saloon was open, but only served coffee and sandwiches until one in the afternoon.

"Yeah, I recognize the both of them," the bartender said. "They was in here maybe two, three times about two weeks ago."

"Did you talk to them at all?" Murphy said.

" 'What will you have? Hello, goodbye.' I'm paid to pour drinks, not socialize with saddle bums."

"What about the ladies?" Murphy said.

"You'd have to ask them," the bartender said. "Wait a minute. I do remember something. They was waiting on a friend. I heard one of them say their friend was late. Something like that."

"They mention a name?" Murphy said.

"Naw."

"Get the ladies down so we can talk to them," Woodward said.

"Angel won't like that," the bartender said.

"Did I ask you what Angel likes?" Woodward said.

The bartender sighed, left the bar, and went up to the second floor.

"Lord help me if Pilar sees me in here," Woodward said.

"She'd understand," Murphy said.

"She's Mexican," Woodward said.

The bartender, followed by Angel, came down the stairs. Angel, a large woman, wore a robe and smoked a cigar.

"Who says I gotta wake my girls early?" Angel said.

"I do," Murphy said.

"You some kind of lawman?" Angel said.

"Just get the girls down here, Angel," Woodward said.

"Gimme ten minutes," Angel said.

Once all eight of Angel's women were seated at a table, Murphy told them why he was there and showed the women the two sketches.

"I could have saved you the trouble," Angel said. "No man sees one of my girls without paying me first. Both of them were here all right. Twice."

"That may be true, but I doubt either of them would make bedroom talk with you in the hallway," Murphy said. "So, ladies, what about it?"

"I saw this one," a blond woman said and pointed to Moats. "Both times."

"Did you talk to him at all?" Murphy said.

"Not much. Just he was waiting on some cowboy," the blond woman said.

"He said that? Cowboy?" Murphy said.

"Mine said that too," a brunette said.

"Are you talking about Skinny?" Angel said.

"He didn't mention no names," the blond said.

"That third night they was at the bar," Angel said. "I saw them from the balcony. Skinny came in and they joined up. Then they all left together."

"Skinny is?" Murphy said.

"I don't know his real name," Angel said. "He's a regular customer. Comes in twice a month for a girl."

"You call him Skinny because?" Murphy said.

"Not because he's fat," Angel said.

"He works at the Amos ranch about fifteen miles west of town," the bartender said.

"Were you here the night he came in and joined the other two?" Murphy said.

The bartender nodded. "They were at the bar and Skinny came in," he said. "One of them said something like, 'It's about damn time,' and then they left."

"Thank you for your time and information," Murphy said.

"Why this Skinny fellow?" Murphy said. "What's the connection between Moats, Holland, and Skinny?"

"We'll ride out to the Amos ranch in the morning," Woodward said. "Go back to your hotel, grab a bath and a nap, and I'll pick you up around six for dinner."

"I have to send a telegram first," Murphy said.

"Murph, this is my oldest boy, Carl Junior, and his brother, Matthew," Woodward said. "Boys, this is Mr. Murphy. We used to work together up in Washington."

"Hello, sir," Carl Junior said.

"Pleased to meet you boys," Murphy said.

"Go wash up for dinner," Pilar said. "Right now."

After dinner, Murphy and Woodward took coffee at the backyard table. It was a warm night, and the sky was filled with stars.

Pilar came out to the table. "The boys want to say good night," she said to Woodward.

"Be right back," Woodward said.

After Woodward entered the house, Pilar took a seat at the table.

"Mr. Murphy, do you love your wife and baby?" Pilar said.

"Very much," Murphy said.

"Then why do you still do this dangerous work?" Pilar said. "Why are you not at home with them right now?"

"This has to be done," Murphy said.

"Put that on your headstone at the cemetery," Pilar said. " 'This had to be done.' "

Woodward returned to the table.

"It's getting late, Carl," Murphy said. "And I need some sleep."

"I'll walk you out," Woodward said.

"Good night, Mrs. Woodward, and thank you for dinner," Murphy said.

At the door, Woodward said, "Meet you at eight o'clock at my office."

"Good night, Carl," Murphy said.

Murphy sat in a chair on the balcony of his hotel room. He had a small glass of bourbon and his pipe.

Pilar's words echoed in his mind. *Put that on your headstone at the cemetery.*

"Not until these bastards hang," he said aloud.

"I have to get lunch ready for Pa and my brothers," Maddie said. "Will you stay and eat with us?"

"Is that an invite?" Woodward said.

"Sure is," Maddie smiled.

"Then set two extra plates," Woodward said.

After Maddie went inside, Murphy said, "Her mother?"

"Died some time ago," Woodward said. "Ned had to raise her and his two boys alone. No easy task while running a ranch."

"Looks like he's done a fine job," Murphy said.

A while later, Maddie walked out to the porch as Amos and her two brothers came riding to the house.

"Hello, Ned," Woodward said.

"Carl, is something wrong?" Ned Amos said as he walked up to the porch.

"Nothing's wrong, Ned. This is Mr. Murphy. He's a federal agent. We have some questions about a man who worked for you," Woodward said.

"Can we talk over lunch?" Amos said.

Woodward looked at Maddie. "It's delicate," he said.

"Maddie, is lunch ready?" Amos said.

"Yes, Pa," Maddie said.

"Then let's eat," Amos said.

After lunch, Woodward, Murphy, Amos, and his two sons gathered at a table in the backyard that was protected from the sun by a cloth awning. Maddie had brought out a pitcher of lemonade and five glasses.

"All we know about the hand we're interested in is that he goes by the name of Skinny," Murphy said.

Amos looked at his oldest son. "Samuel is in charge of the bunkhouse," he said.

"Skinny Johnson," Samuel said. "Came here about five months ago. He's actually a fair hand for so thin a fellow."

"What's his real name?" Murphy said.

"I think it's Steven," Samuel said. "No, Seth. I'm sure of it. Seth."

"Did he say where he's from?" Murphy said.

"Phoenix way," Samuel way. "But when he signed on here, he said he'd been working a spread down in Texas. He said he got homesick."

"Do you know where in Texas?" Murphy said.

"Austin, I think," Samuel said.

"Did he have plans he ever talked about?" Murphy said.

"The men all talk when on the range," Samuel said. "Who's going where and doing what, that kind of thing. Skinny used to say he would go to California and try his hand at gold."

"Gold?" Woodward said.

"He used to say that all the time," Samuel said. "He was going to get a grubstake and go looking for gold."

"He talk about friends off the ranch?" Murphy said.

"Not as I recall," Samuel said.

"What did Skinny do that the federal law is after him?" Amos said.

"Make friends with the wrong people," Murphy said.

"My boys need to get back to work," Amos said.

"Thank you for the information and for the lunch," Murphy said.

Alone on the balcony of his hotel room, Murphy smoked his pipe and sipped from a small glass of bourbon.

Things were beginning to make sense. Moats, Holland, and Skinny Johnson all worked as trail hands at the Bass ranch. As it naturally happens in bunkhouses, the men talked and gossiped and played cards to pass the time.

Moats, Holland, and Johnson talked about striking it rich in California gold. To Johnson, it was probably wishful thinking, but not to Moats and Holland. Homesick for Arizona, Johnson left for home.

Moats and Holland stayed behind and learned about a rich whiskey maker in Tennessee. They got the idea of robbing him to get their grubstake.

Afterward, Moats and Holland headed to Tucson to pick up Johnson before heading to California.

California is a huge state, but there were only certain areas a man could look for gold.

Where to start?

If Johnson was the sort who left Texas to return to Arizona because he was homesick, before heading to California, he would visit his family in Phoenix.

Phoenix was the next stop.

CHAPTER THIRTY-SEVEN

"Say goodbye to Pilar and your boys for me," Murphy said after boarding Boyle in the boxcar.

"I will," Woodward said. "Hey, come visit sometime after you're retired."

"Take care," Murphy said and boarded the train.

Kai and Aideen waited on the porch for the foreman to arrive with the buggy.

"If I come to live with you and my son and the baby, is there enough room for me?" Aideen said.

"The house has six bedrooms," Kai said.

"And what about this house?" Aideen said.

"Let the foreman live here to keep the place up," Kai said. "We'd only be a short buggy ride away, and I'm sure Murphy will be over almost every day to keep an eye on the business."

"But does a married man with a baby wish to have his mother underfoot all the time?" Aideen said.

"I think he will insist on it," Kai said.

The foreman arrived with the buggy. "I'll be back before lunch," Kai said, and she got into the buggy beside the foreman.

The ride to Phoenix took only two and a half hours, and the train arrived before noon. As Murphy walked from the railroad station to Main Street, he noticed it was even hotter and drier in Phoenix than in Tucson.

The temperature was close to a hundred degrees and yet so dry that Murphy didn't sweat as he walked to the center of the small town of two thousand residents.

Phoenix was founded as a farming community, despite the arid and dry climate, thanks to its access to the Salt and Gila Rivers and its canal systems.

So if Skinny Johnson called Phoenix home, it was a safe bet his family were farmers.

Alfalfa, cotton, and citrus were the main crops. Johnson's family probably grew one of them, or even all three.

"Come on, boy, let's find a hotel," Murphy said as he led Boyle along Main Street.

There were three hotels on Front Street, but only one had its own livery and balconies on the third and fourth floors, The Phoenix House. After registering for three days and board for Boyle, Murphy asked about the local sheriff.

He was directed to Harvey's Feed and Grain two blocks down on Front Street.

Murphy left the hotel and walked the three blocks to Harvey's store. It was large and sectioned into three separate areas: one for feed, another for grain, and a third for seed.

At least a dozen wagons littered the street in front of the store. Farmers were loading their wagons with sacks of feed, grain, and seeds. Others were buying farming tools and implements.

Four clerks were assisting customers when Murphy entered the store.

"Can I help you?" a clerk said as he approached Murphy.

"I'm looking for the sheriff," Murphy said.

"The sheriff?" the clerk said.

"I was told he was here," Murphy said.

"He's in the office," the clerk said.

The clerk led Murphy to a door. He knocked and opened the

door. "Someone to see you, Mr. Harvey," he said.

"I'm busy," Harvey said.

"He's . . ." the clerk said as Murphy walked past the clerk, into the office, and closed the door.

At his desk, Harvey was doing paperwork.

"Sheriff Harvey?" Murphy said.

"Part-time," Harvey said. "Who are you?"

Murphy showed his identification to Harvey.

"Is the president coming?" Harvey said.

"Not likely," Murphy said.

"Then why are you here?" Harvey said.

"I have two . . ." Murphy said as the door opened and a clerk stuck his head in.

"Mr. Harvey, we're almost out of . . ." the clerk said.

"Get out," Murphy said and slammed the door closed.

"You were saying?" Harvey said.

"I have two warrants to serve for robbery and murder," Murphy said.

"Why tell me?"

"You're the sheriff, aren't you?"

"Part-time and nonpaid," Harvey said.

"Do you know a fellow they call Skinny Johnson?" Murphy said.

"Since he was ten years old," Harvey said. "You can't have a warrant for him, not that boy."

"No, but he's friends with the two the warrant is intended for," Murphy said. "He hooked up with them in Tucson, and I believe they stopped off here. Can you tell me where I might find his family?"

"Let me see the warrants," Harvey said.

Murphy set them on the desk. Harvey read them and handed them back to Murphy. "Seth Johnson is mixed up with these two?" he said.

169

"Not as a participant," Murphy said. "As a bystander."

"Have you a horse?" Harvey said.

"Do you think I arrived on a bicycle?" Murphy said.

Harvey looked through his desk. "Let me find my badge," he said.

As Harvey led the way to the Johnson farm, he said, "They got a nice five-hundred-acre spread. Grow alfalfa and several kinds of citrus."

"How big a family?" Murphy said.

"Well, there's James and his wife, Emily," Harvey said. "Seth is the oldest boy, followed by Jimmy and then Sarah."

"I take it Seth didn't take to farming," Murphy said.

"That boy always wanted to be a cowboy," Harvey said. "But I suspect he just really hates farming."

They reached a turnoff in the road. Harvey led Murphy to the left. They rode past a hundred acres of alfalfa.

"At the end of this field is the house," Harvey said.

When they reached the end of the field, a large farmhouse, barn, and corral came into view.

A young woman was hanging wash on a line.

"That's Sarah," Harvey said.

As they neared the house, Sarah ran inside and James came on the porch.

"Mr. Harvey, what brings you by?" James said.

"James, we need to talk," Harvey said.

After Emily served coffee on the porch, Murphy explained the reason for the visit.

"My son is wanted for murder?" James said.

"Oh, my God," Emily said.

"No," Murphy said. "At the present time, I'm sure he has no idea of the character of the men he's riding with."

"None of this makes sense," James said. "Seth always hated farming and wanted to work with horses."

"These men, what do they want with my son?" Emily said.

"I think their intention was to steal enough money to get a grubstake for a claim in California," Murphy said. "They figure the law is looking for two, not three, so they picked up your son as a guise."

"Which puts my son in terrible danger," Emily said.

"You don't know that," James said.

"Those men are wanted for murder, James," Emily said. "If it comes down to it and they have to, they'll kill our boy."

"Is that right, Mr. Murphy? They'll kill our boy?" James said.

Next to Emily, Sarah started to cry. Emily put her arm around her.

"Right now they have no notion I'm on their trail," Murphy said. "If I can get to them before it becomes necessary, I can save your son."

"You don't even know where they went," James said.

"I do," Sarah said.

Everybody looked at Sarah.

"How do you know?" James said.

"I heard them talking from my window when they thought everyone was asleep the night they stayed over," Sarah said. "The two men said they wanted to stop in Reno to do some gambling before they went to California."

"Reno," Murphy said.

"That's what they said," Sarah said. "I heard them plain as day."

"Mr. Murphy, find them. Save our boy," Emily said.

"I'd better head back to town," Murphy said. "Reno is a long way, and I'll need to take the train."

"Mr. Murphy, you didn't answer me," Emily said. "Will you save our boy?"

"I will do what I can," Murphy said. "That I promise."

"I should go with you," James said.

"No," Murphy said.

"Seth is my son," James said.

"Mr. Johnson, a good way to get your boy killed is to put the backs of these two men against the wall," Murphy said. "Have you ever fired a gun at a man? It's not the same thing as shooting rabbits or the occasional deer. This is a job for the law. If you want your son back alive, you'll leave it to the law."

"He's right, James," Emily said.

James nodded. "Will you let us know about our son?" he said.

"When I can," Murphy said.

"Does this town have a decent steak?" Murphy said as he and Harvey dismounted at the hotel.

"Arizona is cattle country, Mr. Murphy," Harvey said. "You'll find the restaurant in your hotel serves as fine a beef as anywhere."

"Thanks."

Murphy walked Boyle to the hotel and took him into the livery. "Feed him as much grain and water as he wants. And for God's sake, don't try to brush him. He'll stomp you to death if you come at him with a brush."

At the front desk, Murphy asked to have a steak dinner delivered to his room, then went to his room to relax.

Harvey was right; the steak was excellent.

After eating, Murphy took his pipe and a glass of bourbon to the balcony. The temperature had dropped to a manageable seventy degrees.

He sat in a chair and thought about Reno.

CHAPTER THIRTY-EIGHT

After breakfast, Murphy checked out of the hotel and walked Boyle to the railroad station to buy a ticket to Reno.

The train wouldn't arrive until noon, so he had three hours to fill. After buying his ticket, Murphy rode to Harvey's store, which was full of customers again. Murphy found Harvey in his office.

"Leaving for Reno?" Harvey said.

"Noon train."

"Are you going to do what you said about the Johnson boy?" Harvey said.

"That's up to the Johnson boy," Murphy said. "Right now he's riding with two dangerous and wanted men. If he chooses to surrender, there will be no charges against him. But if he takes their side, I make no promises about the outcome."

"I'll keep that information to myself," Harvey said.

"Appreciate it," Murphy said.

After leaving Harvey, Murphy went to the telegraph office and sent a wire to Kai.

Murphy booked a sleeping car, even though the train was scheduled to arrive in Reno at three in the morning. After boarding Boyle in the boxcar, he went to his car and took a short nap to refresh himself.

Dinner was served between six and eight. Around seven p.m., Murphy went to the dining car and ordered the baked chicken.

away from the main boulevard that the music didn't reach its front doors. It also had a livery.

A sleepy clerk told Murphy the going rate for a room was ten dollars a night, paid in advance.

"Ten dollars? I could get a suite in San Francisco for ten dollars," Murphy said.

"No doubt," the clerk said. "Do you want the room or not?"

"For three days. How much for my horse to be stabled?" Murphy said.

"Five dollars a night," the clerk said.

"You're kidding."

"You could catch the train to San Francisco," the clerk said.

"No doubt," Murphy said as he paid the clerk forty-five dollars.

After a quiet breakfast in the hotel restaurant, which cost five dollars, Murphy ventured out on foot to Main Street.

The side streets were lined with homes that could have been located in any town, anywhere, but when he reached Main Street, everything changed.

Every casino and saloon was open and crowded. Music sounded from all of them. The streets were filled with buggies and wagons, pedestrians and cowboys.

Deputies seemed to be everywhere, armed with sidearms and rifles.

Murphy approached a deputy. "Can you tell me where I can find the sheriff?" he said.

"That depends on who's doing the asking," the deputy said.

Murphy took out his wallet and showed his identification to the deputy.

"Follow me," the deputy said.

Murphy walked beside the deputy for several blocks until they reached the Taste of Reno restaurant. They entered and walked to a table where the sheriff was having breakfast.

"Sheriff, this man wants a word with you," the deputy said.

Sheriff J. Coffey looked up at Murphy. "Who are you, and what do you want?" he said.

Murphy tossed his wallet on the table. "Murphy, United States Secret Service," he said.

"Take a chair," Coffey said.

Murphy sat opposite Coffey. "Want some breakfast?" Coffey said.

"I already ate, but I'll take a cup of coffee," Murphy said.

Coffey waved to a waitress. "Mabel, coffee for the gentleman," Coffey said.

The waitress put a full cup on the table.

"So, is the president coming?" Coffey said.

"No."

"So why are you here?" Coffey said.

"I have two warrants for men who committed murder. They apparently came to your town," Murphy said.

Coffey looked at Murphy. "Murder, you say?" he said.

Murphy produced the two warrants and showed them to Coffey.

"How do you know they came here?" Coffey said.

"They said so," Murphy said.

"How long ago?"

"Maybe ten days or less."

"You think they're still here?"

Murphy took out the sketches and showed them to Coffey. "Our resident population is around three thousand," Coffey said. "On any given weeknight we get two, three thousand cowboys, miners, and gamblers. On Saturday, maybe four thousand. Some comes from as far away as Sacramento, thanks to the railroad. Do you really think I would remember the faces of two strangers?"

"They picked up a kid from Phoenix," Murphy said. "A thin fellow they call Skinny. I'd like to . . ."

"A skinny fellow, you say? Answers to the name Johnson?" Coffey said.

"Yes. Do you know where he is?" Murphy said.

"I know exactly where that fellow is," Coffey said.

"Well?" Murphy said.

"Right after I finish my breakfast," Coffey said.

Reno had a nice jail and courthouse, and holding cells in the sheriff's office. Coffey had his deputies bring Johnson to the holding cells.

"What did he do?" Murphy said.

"Him and, I guess, his two wanted companions were playing cards at the Pig and Whistle Casino," Coffey said. "He got into it with one of the players. The man pulled a knife. Johnson pulled a .45 derringer. The player stabbed Johnson in the arm. Johnson shot the player in the leg. We arrested them both for violation of the no-firearms-in-casinos policy. They each got thirty days."

"How long ago?" Murphy said.

At his desk, Coffey checked the arrest log. "Nine days ago today."

A deputy came in from the back room. "That skinny fellow is in a back cell, Sheriff," he said.

"Come on," Coffey said.

Murphy followed Coffey to the back room where six cells were located. Only one cell was occupied. By Skinny Johnson.

"Open the door," Murphy said.

Coffey unlocked the cell door, and he and Murphy entered. Skinny Johnson sat on his cot and looked up at Murphy.

"Are you my lawyer?" Johnson said.

"Murphy, United States Secret Service," Murphy said.

"I never heard of no secret service," Johnson said. "Guess it's cause it's a secret."

Murphy smacked Johnson so hard that he fell off the cot and landed on his face.

"Mouth off to me again, boy, and, I'll leave you in here," Murphy said.

Coffey, a half-foot shorter than Murphy, looked up at him.

"Get up," Murphy said.

Johnson slowly got to his feet with blood running from his nose and mouth.

"Sit down," Murphy said.

Johnson sat on the cot. "You didn't have to do that," he said. "I was just funning."

"Your two friends are going to hang for murder," Murphy said. "You could spend twenty years in Yuma prison for accessory after the fact."

"What the hell are you talking about?" Johnson said. "All I did was defend myself against a card cheat who pulled a knife."

"Can you read?" Murphy said.

"Of course I can read," Johnson said.

"Read this," Murphy said and handed the warrants to Johnson.

As Johnson read, all color drained from his face. He looked up at Murphy. "I didn't know. How was I to know any of this?" he said.

"When did you last bathe?" Murphy said.

"I guess it's been ten days now."

"Sheriff, have him cleaned up, then bring him a steak. After that we'll have a nice talk," Murphy said.

Coffey looked at Murphy.

"That wasn't a request," Murphy said.

Clean and shaven, Johnson ate a steak while Murphy and Cof-

"Those men could be anywhere by now," Murphy said. "I have little chance of picking up their trail from here. I need to show that kid he's been lied to and used. It's the only way he'll really come clean."

"I'll speak to the judge and arrange for his bail and release," Coffey said.

"I should accompany you and present the warrants and state my need for his release," Murphy said.

"Where can I reach you?"

"At my hotel," Murphy said.

Murphy was in the hotel bathing room, soaking in a hot tub, when there was a knock on the door.

"Yes," Murphy said.

"It's Sheriff Coffey."

Murphy stood and wrapped a towel around his waist. "Enter," he said.

Coffey opened the door and walked in. "I spoke to the . . ." he said and paused when he saw the bullet wounds and knife scars on Murphy's chest, shoulders, and arms.

"Continue," Murphy said.

"The judge. He'll see us at ten tomorrow morning," Coffey said.

"Join me for a steak tonight," Murphy said.

"The Reno Café on Main Street serves the best in town," Coffey said.

"Seven o'clock," Murphy said.

CHAPTER FORTY

Murphy had to admit the steak was as good as any he'd had in the big cities of New York and Chicago.

"Raised on Nevada grass," Coffey said.

"Which saloon served the best bourbon?" Murphy said.

"Probably the Pig and Whistle," Coffey said.

"I suggest a nightcap," Murphy said.

A deputy was posted on the sidewalk to make sure every man entering the Pig and Whistle checked their guns on the gun rack by the door.

"Evening, Sheriff," the deputy said.

"This is Mr. Murphy. He is with me and allowed to keep his firearm," Coffey said.

The Pig and Whistle Saloon and gambling hall rivaled any in Saint Louis, Kansas City, or San Francisco. It was wall-to-wall splendor, with gaming tables, mirrors, a piano and banjo player, and women servers.

Every gaming table was occupied. The bar was standing room only. Four burly bouncers patrolled the room with eyes on the gaming tables.

A lone table against the rear wall was unoccupied. Coffey led Murphy to the table.

"This table is reserved for me and my deputies should the need arise and we have to keep watch," Coffey said.

As soon as they took chairs, a waitress arrived.

"Two of your best bourbons," Coffey said.

She nodded and walked to the bar.

"I heard from a reliable source that the bar alone makes five thousand a night," Coffey said. "The house take from the tables is five percent of the winnings, and who knows what the ladies upstairs bring."

The waitress returned with two glasses of bourbon and two glasses of water on the side. "Do you want a tab, Sheriff?" she said.

"We're just having the one," Coffey said.

She nodded and walked away. Murphy and Coffey sampled the bourbon. "Not bad," Murphy said.

"Question for you, Mr. Murphy," Coffey said. "Suppose you prove to Johnson in Sacramento that no claim has been filed, what then?"

"I'm hoping to shame him into giving up the location where Moats and Holland went," Murphy said.

"And if he isn't shamed?"

"I'll turn him loose and hope he leads me to them."

"That's quite a risk."

"What choice do I have?" Murphy said. "I've been trailing these men from Tennessee to Texas to Arkansas to here. If I don't find them soon, I fear I never will."

"I understand your position, but . . ."

From outside the saloon, a man shouted, "Outta my way, Deputy, or get shot."

A gunshot sounded and then a man armed with a revolver rushed into the saloon. "Where's the crooked, thieving sumbitch faro dealer at?" he shouted.

The music stopped and all gazes turned upon the man.

"There you are, you sumbitch," the man said. He cocked the revolver and walked toward a faro table. He stopped and aimed.

Murphy jumped up, drew his Colt, cocked, and fired. The

bullet struck the man in the center of his chest, and he fell dead to the floor.

Everyone stared at Murphy. "Better see to your deputy outside," he said.

Murphy and Coffey waited in the doctor's office for news on the deputy.

"The bartender measured your shot at ninety-three feet," Coffey said. "And my guess is that was no lucky shot."

The back door opened and the doctor walked out. "Your man lost a lot of blood, but he's stabilized and will recover in time," he said.

"Thank God for that," Coffey said.

The doctor looked at Murphy. "You're the man who killed that lunatic in the saloon," he said.

"It was necessary," Murphy said.

"When can I see my deputy?" Coffey said.

"Tomorrow," the doctor said.

"Mr. Murphy, I propose we finish our drink in my office," Coffey said.

Coffey filled two shot glasses with bourbon and gave one to Murphy.

"To good shooting," Coffey said.

They tossed back their shots, then Murphy said, "I'll see you in the morning."

In his hotel room, Murphy took pen to paper and wrote Kai a detailed letter. In the letter he asked her to tell Harry, upon his return, to go to Reno, Nevada, as they could do quite well selling bourbon in that environment.

He went to sleep and didn't think once about the man he

killed that night. Killing that man had saved another.
That is how a lawman gets through the day.

CHAPTER FORTY-ONE

Murphy met Coffey at nine-thirty at Coffey's office. Together they walked to the redbrick courthouse on Main Street.

The judge listened to Murphy's case, read the warrants, and then said, "I will release Mr. Johnson to your custody and hope he leads you to a successful conclusion."

"Thank you, Your Honor," Murphy said.

"A moment, Mr. Murphy," the judge said.

"Yes, Your Honor," Murphy said.

"I spent some time as a judge in Washington," the judge said. "Might you be the Murphy who headed up President Grant's personal security detail?"

"I am," Murphy said.

Coffey looked at Murphy.

"The same Murphy who recently brought to justice the repeat killer who terrorized New York City and also foiled a counterfeit money ring designed to ruin the economy?" the judge said. "And also solved many a crisis for Judge Parker in Fort Smith?"

Murphy nodded.

"Have dinner with me tonight, Mr. Murphy," the judge said. "Seven o'clock at my residence."

"Thank you, Judge," Murphy said.

"My carriage will pick you up at your hotel at six-thirty," the judge said.

As they left the courthouse, Coffey said, "I see how you

187

earned all those scars."

"Let's go talk to Johnson," Murphy said.

"I travel with you to Sacramento to check on their claim, and if it ain't there, you'll bring me back to Reno and set me free. Is that it?" Johnson said.

"That's it," Murphy said.

"And if there is a claim filed?" Johnson said.

"I put you on the train back to Reno. Sheriff Coffey will meet you at the station and give you your horse and gun back," Murphy said. "And pay for a train ticket back to Phoenix. All charges against you will be dropped."

"Mr. Murphy, you got yourself a deal," Johnson said.

"Sit tight tonight, and we'll leave in the morning," Murphy said.

After a deputy returned Johnson to his holding cell, Coffey said, "I hope you know what you're doing."

"So do I," Murphy said.

Murphy had time to freshen up and change his shirt before the judge's carriage picked him up at six-thirty.

Murphy was met at the front door of the judge's very exclusive home by the judge himself.

"Dinner is at seven, so we have time to whet our appetite with a small glass of brandy," the judge said.

In the judge's den, he served two small glasses of brandy. Murphy kept his distaste for brandy to himself and sipped the God-awful concoction slowly.

"My wife passed away five years ago," the judge said. "I'd had enough of Washington and decided to move west and try something new, so to speak. But I still keep track of what goes on. That's how I recognized your name."

A black woman of about sixty entered the den. "Supper's

ready, Judge," she said.

"We'll be along, Esther," the judge said.

Esther nodded and left the den.

"Esther's been with me since fifty-nine, when she escaped to Boston on the Underground Railroad," the judge said. "I was a young lawyer then, married with two sons, and we hired her to be our housekeeper. I don't know what I would have done without her. I still don't."

"Whatever she's cooking smells delicious," Murphy said.

"Let's go find out," the judge said.

Esther served baked hens with roasted potatoes, carrots, and corn. She served red wine to drink.

"I have to admit, she's worth her weight in gold," Murphy said.

"This boy Johnson. How sure are you he knows the location of those two murderers?" the judge said.

"I'd bet a case of bourbon on it," Murphy said.

"A case, huh?" the judge said. "As much as I'd like to take that bet, I happen to agree with your assessment of Johnson's character."

"He comes from a decent family in Phoenix," Murphy said. "His situation is not one of circumstance, but self-made."

"I can't tell you how many men I've sentenced to prison who came from decent families," the judge said.

Esther entered the dining room. "Desert and coffee are ready in the parlor," she said.

Dessert was chocolate cake with white frosting that was as good as any Murphy had eaten anywhere.

Before leaving, Murphy made a point to compliment Esther and thank her for dinner.

"My carriage will take you back to your hotel," the judge said. "And good luck tomorrow."

CHAPTER FORTY-TWO

The eight o'clock train would get Murphy and Johnson to Sacramento by ten in the morning.

Murphy didn't bother to handcuff Johnson. He put him in a window seat and sat next to him to block the aisle.

"Mind a question?" Johnson said.

"Go ahead," Murphy said.

"Why are you so sure they didn't file a claim?" Johnson said.

"They're thieves and murderers, and they stole a great deal of money before they got to Reno," Murphy said. "They're not going to break their backs panning for gold when they've got all that money in their pockets."

"You're wrong, and I'll prove it in Sacramento," Johnson said.

"We'll find out soon enough," Murphy said.

As the capital of California, Sacramento was a thriving city of twenty-five-thousand residents. Buildings were mostly brick and modern. As the home of the Gold Rush of forty-nine, the city had considerable wealth.

From the railroad station, Murphy and Johnson took a taxi to the government building in downtown Sacramento that recorded claims and deeds.

Firearms weren't allowed inside the building, so Murphy had to check his Colt in the lobby with a Sacramento police officer.

They spent several hours researching claims filed during the past thirty days. They found none registered to either Moats or Holland.

"Convinced, kid?" Murphy said.

"They were going to leave me there in jail," Johnson said.

"Not 'going to.' They did," Murphy said.

"I can't believe it," Johnson said. "I thought they were my friends."

"They're murderers. They don't have friends," Murphy said.

"Now what?" Johnson said.

"I'm putting you back on the train to Reno," Murphy said. "You'll be met by Sheriff Coffey and put up for the night. In the morning, you'll be given your horse and gun back."

"How do you know you can trust me?" Johnson said.

"Do you want your horse and gun, or for Coffey to keep them?" Murphy said.

Johnson nodded. " 'Course I want them back," he said. "I'll need them in Phoenix."

"The train back doesn't leave until four. If you're hungry, let's have us a late lunch," Murphy said.

They found a small restaurant near the train station.

Johnson picked at his food.

"Don't feel so bad about it, kid," Murphy said. "Sooner or later, they'll be caught. If you were with them, you'd have to pay for their crimes. It's bad enough to pay for crimes you do. It's worse to pay for the crimes of others."

"I didn't think of that," Johnson said. "I guess you are right."

"I've been a lawman long enough to know I am right," Murphy said. "You've been given a second chance with a clean slate. Take advantage of it."

Johnson nodded. "I will," he said.

Murphy shook hands with Johnson before the young man boarded the train.

"Why are you staying in Sacramento?" Johnson said.

"Just because they didn't file a claim doesn't mean they didn't stop here," Murphy said. "I have to be sure before I move on."

Johnson nodded and then boarded the train.

Once Johnson was aboard, Murphy walked to the front of the train and climbed up with the engineer.

"Riding with the engineer? You government men sure have strange ways," the engineer said.

"We do what is necessary," Murphy said.

Fifteen minutes later, the engineer pulled the train out of the station. To keep from getting bored during the three-hour ride, Murphy took the place of the assistant engineer and fed coal into the furnace.

Kai exited the post office with a stack of mail and returned to the buggy, where the foreman waited.

"I need to stop at the general store before we head home," Kai said.

"Yes, ma'am," the foreman said.

In wasn't until after dinner that Kai and Aideen opened the mail at the kitchen table. Kai opened the letter from Murphy first.

"He's in Reno," Kai said. "He says to tell Harry that he's to head to Reno when possible. He says it's a great place to sell the bourbon."

"Reno?" Aideen said. "Never heard of it."

Kai reviewed the orders Harry had sent from Saint Louis. They were quite good.

"He's in Columbus now," Kai said. "At the Columbus Hotel."

"If I'm to live with you, where will Harry stay between trips?" Aideen said.

"All he need do is pick a bedroom," Kai said.

★　★　★　★　★

From the engine car, Murphy watched Johnson meet Coffey on the platform. He waited until they left the platform to leave the car.

Then he took a taxi to his hotel.

Murphy removed his jacket and shirt, poured a glass of whiskey, and took his pipe out to the balcony.

By the time Coffey showed up, the streets were dark and lanterns illuminated the main boulevards.

Murphy put on a clean shirt and opened the door when Coffey knocked.

"Had dinner?" Murphy said.

"I have not," Coffey said.

"We can eat right downstairs," Murphy said.

They settled at a table. Steaks ordered, Coffey said, "I put Johnson up at the Charter Hotel and left a deputy in the lobby. At ten o'clock tomorrow, I give him his horse and sidearm and turn him loose."

"Think he'll get on the train back to Phoenix?" Murphy said.

"No. Do you?"

"I'm counting on not," Murphy said. "He knows a great deal more than he lets on, the little shit."

"I can have two of my deputies ride with you," Coffey said.

"Do they have any jurisdiction outside of Reno?" Murphy said.

"They do not," Coffey said.

"Then I can't use them," Murphy said.

"I hope you know what you're doing," Coffey said.

"I hope Johnson knows where he's going," Murphy said.

CHAPTER FORTY-THREE

Murphy waited in the lobby of a small hotel across the street from the Charter Hotel and watched as Coffey handed Johnson the reins of his horse.

They shook hands, and then Johnson mounted the saddle.

Once Johnson was out of sight, Murphy walked outside and crossed the street to Coffey.

"Did you have the blacksmith change out the rear right shoe?" Murphy said.

"This morning," Coffey said.

"Your deputies?" Murphy said.

"On the street, watching his direction."

"I'll give him two hours," Murphy said.

"Stop by the office before you go, and I'll give you my deputies' report," Coffey said.

Murphy went to his hotel, packed his saddlebags with clean clothes from the hotel's laundry, and then retrieved Boyle from the stable.

He walked Boyle to the general store on Front Street and purchased a week's worth of supplies. Then he walked Boyle to Coffey's office.

"All set?" Coffey said.

"Just about," Murphy said.

"Well, you were right," Coffey said. "He rode right past the railroad and headed southeast out of town."

"Obliged for everything, Sheriff," Murphy said. "I hope to get back here one day."

A deputy was posted at the railroad. Murphy dismounted to speak with him.

"He rode southeast," the deputy said. "You can't miss his tracks, with the one shoe different."

Murphy inspected the tracks. The rear right shoe had a star pattern the other three shoes did not.

"What's southeast of here?" Murphy said.

"Carson City is about thirty miles. After that, Lake Tahoe," the deputy said.

"Thanks."

"Good luck."

Murphy followed the tracks away from the railroad. After several miles, he was in deep pine-tree country. The grass was lush, and Johnson's tracks were simple enough to follow.

After two hours of easy riding, Murphy dismounted to check the tracks in the loose dirt. They were Johnson's, and he was still on course for Carson City.

But he wouldn't make thirty miles traveling at the pace he was keeping before dark. He'd camp and ride into Carson City sometime around noon.

Murphy kept pace so that he was two hours behind Johnson. He could have easily overtaken him, but he needed Johnson to lead him to Moats and Holland.

Close to dark, he stopped and made camp. Using his rain poncho, Murphy constructed a wall to his campfire, as fire can be seen from a great distance at night. After putting beans and bacon and a pot of coffee on the fire, Murphy tended to Boyle.

Once Boyle was happy, Murphy sat down with his back against the saddle to eat. He had fresh cornbread from the general store in Reno, and carved out a large piece to go with the beans and bacon.

After eating, Murphy filled a cup with coffee and added an ounce of bourbon from his flask and watched the dark horizon.

He saw a tiny red speck in the distance.

Johnson's campfire.

It was still visible when Murphy went to sleep.

After breakfast, Kai and Aideen took the baby to the porch for some morning sunshine. The baby was getting restless now, wanting to walk, and it was harder to keep her at bay when she wanted to stand.

As they drank coffee with the morning sun on their faces, a dust cloud appeared on the road.

They knew it wasn't Harry. Then the buggy came into view and they saw the buggy contained William Burke.

"Do you want to shoot him, or should I?" Kai said.

"Hear what he has to say first," Aideen said.

Burke drove his buggy past the gate and stopped at the porch. "Kai, Mrs. Murphy, may I dismount without buckshot flying my way?" he said.

"Come ahead, you old fool," Kai said.

Burke climbed down from the buggy and went up to the porch. "May I take a chair?" he said.

"You buffoon, sit down and I'll bring you a cup of coffee," Kai said.

"Thank you kindly," Burke said.

Kai went inside and returned a few moments later with a cup of coffee and handed it to Burke.

"What does the president want this time?" Kai said.

"I am here of my own accord," Burke said. "For several reasons. First, I had the opportunity to see Grant last week when I had to be in New York. He wrote this letter and asked me to deliver it to you."

196

"Why couldn't he mail it?" Aideen said.

"He knew I was coming down here and asked me to deliver it personally," Burke said. "He apologized for not attending the services for Mr. Murphy, but he's too ill to travel."

"We understand," Aideen said.

"You said several reasons," Kai said.

"True," Burke said. "I am searching for a place to retire. Tennessee might suit my purpose."

"What purpose is that?" Kai said.

"Warm summers and mild winters," Burke said.

"You could do worse," Kai said.

"What of Murphy?" Burke said.

"He's in Reno, last I heard," Kai said.

"So he's onto something?" Burke said.

"Well, he didn't go there to admire the pine trees," Kai said. "Will you be staying the night?"

"If I'm invited," Burke said.

"I'll fix up a room, you old fool," Kai said.

After a breakfast of coffee and a few biscuits from the general store, Murphy continued following Johnson's tracks.

He reached Johnson's campsite within two hours. The ashes from the fire were still warm.

Johnson was still on track for Carson City. Even at his slow pace, he would reach it by noon.

"Let's go, boy," Murphy said. "Nice and easy. We don't want to alert Johnson we're on his trail."

A moment later, a powerful blow to the left temple threw Murphy from Boyle. As he lay bleeding on the ground, Murphy heard Johnson yell, "Got you, you son of a bitch!"

CHAPTER FORTY-FOUR

The bullet didn't penetrate Murphy's skin, but it felt as if a mule kicked him in the head. Blood from his temple ran into Murphy's left eye, blinding it. He tried to move, but was overcome by dizziness.

Murphy heard Johnson's footsteps approaching. "Did you think I believed all your bullshit?" he said. "I knew you'd follow me, lawman. You can't help yourself. But did you really think I'd betray my friends for the likes of you? Fat fucking chance of that happening."

Murphy felt a rope fall around his neck. He grabbed it with his hands.

"Gonna hang you and leave you for the buzzards, lawman," Johnson said. "Maybe some drunk Indians will find you and stick you in the ground."

Murphy turned and watched as Johnson walked to his horse. Just as Johnson put his foot in the stirrup, Murphy yanked hard on the rope, knocking Johnson to the ground.

"Son of a bitch," Johnson yelled.

Murphy reached for his Colt and cocked it.

Johnson jumped to his feet and pulled his sidearm. "I'll kill you, law dog," he yelled and walked to Murphy.

Dizzy, disoriented, and half blind from blood, Murphy fired his Colt, and Johnson was blown over backward.

Murphy whistled for Boyle and the horse came to Murphy's

side. "Need a little help, boy," Murphy said as he holstered the Colt.

He grabbed the reins and slowly pulled himself to his feet, then balanced himself against Boyle's powerful neck.

Johnson was bleeding heavily from a gunshot wound in his upper left chest. He was unconscious, but still alive.

On unsteady legs, Murphy walked to Johnson's horse and slowly walked him to Johnson.

Very carefully, so that he didn't fall over from vertigo, Murphy lifted Johnson and tossed him over the saddle. Then he removed the rope from around his neck and tied Johnson's arms and legs under his horse's belly.

"All right. Okay," Murphy said. He walked to Boyle, removed his own rope, tied it around Johnson's horse's neck, and then mounted the saddle. He tied the other end of the rope around the saddle horn.

"Let's go, Boyle," Murphy said. "Take us to Carson City."

"That was a wonderful lunch," Burke said.

Kai and Burke were having coffee on the porch.

"Tell me something, Burke. Is my husband really free after this?" Kai said.

"Free of his service to the president, yes," Burke said. "Free of his extraordinary talents, no. He will never be free of them because his conscience guides him. That is an amazing gift for a man to have, don't you think?"

Kai looked at Burke and nodded as his words rang true.

Murphy was only vaguely aware of the commotion he was causing as he rode Boyle along Main Street in Carson City.

Through the crowd, a sheriff and a deputy took Boyle's reins.

"Sweet Jesus," the deputy said.

"Murphy. US Secret Service," Murphy said. "This man is my prisoner."

With that, Murphy fell off Boyle into the arms of the sheriff.

"What about you, Burke?" Kai said. "All those years serving presidents. All that power and influence, can you turn it off as easily as turning off a spigot?"

"That power you speak of was never mine," Burke said. "It was only borrowed from those who have it so I could do their bidding."

"So you're content to sit on the porch, watch the sunset, and drink bourbon the rest of your days?" Kai said.

"I thought I might learn the whiskey-making business," Burke said.

Kai stared at Burke for many seconds. Then her lips formed a smile and she laughed.

"You old skunk," she said.

When Murphy opened his eyes, he was in a bed and his head was bandaged.

A woman said, "He's awake, Doctor."

The doctor stepped into the room and stood over Murphy. "Yes, he is, nurse," the doctor said.

"My prisoner?" Murphy said.

"If you mean the young man I took the bullet out of two days ago, he's in the next room," the doctor said.

"Two days ago," Murphy said.

"That's how long you've been asleep," the doctor said.

"I have to see my prisoner," Murphy said and attempted to rise.

The doctor placed his hand on Murphy's chest. "You might be a great and powerful beast, Mr. Murphy, but you are in no condition to get up at the moment. You have a concussion where the bullet struck you. A fraction of an inch to the right and we wouldn't be having this conversation."

"And my prisoner?" Murphy said.

"He'll recover in time," the doctor said. "Do you feel able to eat or drink?"

Murphy nodded. "After two days, I ought to be," he said.

"I'll have the nurse bring you some broth," the doctor said.

"Broth?"

"I'm Sheriff James Hale of Carson City, Mr. Murphy," Hale said. "And from what I've been able to piece together, you have a federal warrant for two men, of whom the man in the next room is neither."

"His name is Seth Johnson, from Phoenix," Murphy said. "I didn't know at the time of the warrant that Johnson was part of it."

"Would you like a cup of coffee?" Hale said.

"I'd like some steak and eggs, is what I would like," Murphy said. "And I don't want to hear any nonsense about broth."

"I'll ask the doc," Hale said. "In the meantime, finish telling me what happened."

Murphy picked up the story from Austin and ended with the ambush on the trail. "My memory is a bit foggy on the details of entering Carson City, but that's about the gist of it."

"I'd say that skinny cowboy is in some deep trouble," Hale said.

"He doesn't know the half of it yet," Murphy said. "Where's that doctor? I want to get out of here."

"I'll get him," Hale said.

Hale went out and the doctor came in. "The sheriff said you're anxious to leave us," he said.

"There are two murderers out there, and the kid in the next room is going to help me get them," Murphy said.

"Not for a week, he's not," the doctor said.

"My head isn't that bad, Doctor. I can—" Murphy said.

"Maybe you can, but he can't," the doctor said. "Not for at least a week."

"What the hell am I supposed to do for a week?" Murphy said.

"Get better," the doctor said.

"I'd get better quicker with a steak and some eggs in me," Murphy said.

CHAPTER FORTY-FIVE

From his hotel room overlooking the main thoroughfare of Carson City, Murphy sat at the desk and wrote a letter to Kai. Earlier he'd sent a telegram, but he felt the need to write more than could be said in a short wire.

He paused when there was a knock on the door. He left the desk to answer the door. It was the doctor.

"Since you won't come to me, I decided to come to you," the doctor said.

"I'm feeling pretty good, Doc," Murphy said.

"Why don't we let me judge that," the doctor said. "Have a seat on the bed."

Murphy sat and the doctor opened his medical bag. Then he got to work examining Murphy. After about twenty minutes, the doctor said, "Heart, lungs, reflexes all excellent, Mr. Murphy. However, I detect a slight trace of the concussion lingering. I'd guess a slight dizziness when getting out of bed and bending over."

"A bit. Not much," Murphy said. "It's hardly noticeable."

"Another day or two, and it should fade," the doctor said.

"About Johnson," Murphy said.

"In three days, he'll be fit enough to travel," the doctor said. "By train, not horseback."

"He won't need his horse," Murphy said. "When can I see him?"

"Today if you like," the doctor said.

A deputy was posted outside Johnson's room at the doctor's office. Johnson was chained to a brass bed by shackles around his left ankle.

"I don't know how I missed you at twenty-five yards," Johnson said.

Murphy turned his face to show the ugly cut on his forehead. "You didn't miss," Murphy said.

"You're a tough bastard, I'll give you that," Johnson said.

"We'll see how tough you are, Johnson, when they put a rope around your neck," Murphy said.

"You are so full of shit," Johnson said. "I've robbed nobody, killed nobody, and you have no proof I was anywhere near Moats and Holland when they killed that man."

"Attempted murder of a federal officer and aiding and abetting two fugitives for starters," Murphy said. "When we reach Fort Smith, I'll see you hang."

"Fort Smith?" Johnson said.

"Heard of Judge Parker?" Murphy said. "They call him the hanging judge. He's a close, personal friend of mine. He'll try your case and hang you quick as you please, and then he and I will go out for apple pie and coffee."

Johnson stared at Murphy.

"Have a sweet night, Johnson," Murphy said. "You won't be enjoying many more."

"Nice town you got here, Sheriff," Murphy said. "A lot different than Reno."

"You'd expect a more civilized atmosphere from the capital

of Nevada," Earl said. "The politicians won't allow it to be otherwise."

They were having dinner in the restaurant of Murphy's hotel.

"It's quite a modern place, Carson City," Murphy said. "In walking around, I've seen churches, schools, and even a college. I've seen electric lights in several locations, and my guess is the telephone will be here in the near future."

"Talk by the town council is that, within the next three years, the governor will have a phone," Earl said.

"Before I forget, we'd best talk about Johnson's horse. He won't be needing it," Murphy said. "He seems a decent enough mount. Maybe you can use him or sell him, but he won't be making the trip to Fort Smith in two days."

"We can always find a use for a good horse," Earl said.

"That reminds me. Mine can use some exercise," Murphy said. "Where do you suggest I take him out tomorrow?"

"Head southwest and ride along the Carson River," Earl said. "It's a right pretty ride to stretch your legs."

"Feel like a nightcap?" Murphy said.

"The Carson Saloon has the best whiskey in town," Hale said. "Sometimes even the governor stops by."

As Murphy and Hale walked along a wood sidewalk to the Carson Saloon, a deputy stopped them.

"Sheriff, the governor wants to see you," the deputy said.

"Now? Is there a problem?" Hale said.

"He said to tell you he'd like to have a drink with you and Mr. Murphy in his private residence," the deputy said.

Although he was governor of Nevada, a western state, Governor Jewett Adams spoke with a distinct New England accent, as he was born and raised in Vermont. He came west as a young man for the Gold Rush in 1851, and his accent came with him.

He was of average height and had a great sloping mustache.

Adams met Hale and Murphy in the den of his private residence.

"I must admit my curiosity got the better of me when I heard about you, Mr. Murphy," Adams said. "It isn't often a secret service agent rides through town, especially the way you did."

"Believe me, Governor, that wasn't a planned entrance," Murphy said.

"I expect not," Adams said. "Well gentlemen, name your poison. I'm partial to bourbon myself."

"That will do fine," Murphy said.

Adams poured three small glasses of bourbon and passed one to Murphy and Hale. "To your good health," Adams said.

Each man took a small sip.

"When will you be leaving us, Mr. Murphy?" Adams said.

"Day after tomorrow if Johnson is fit enough," Murphy said.

"And the other two men you seek, are they still in Nevada?" Adams said.

"They could be anywhere, but maybe," Murphy said. "I will have copies of their sketches made for Hale and his deputies."

Adams nodded. "I sent some telegrams to Washington," he said. "As I said, for my own curiosity. I was told that in some circles you are called the President's Regulator."

Murphy grinned. "I've been called a lot of things, Governor, most of them not good," he said.

"I hope when your business is concluded that you come back and see us," Adams said. "Ours is a growing town. I expect to have a telephone in three years."

At Murphy's hotel, Hale said, "The President's Regulator."

"Catchy, isn't it?" Murphy said.

"Have a good ride tomorrow," Hale said.

CHAPTER FORTY-SIX

Burke drove the wagon to town so Kai could get the mail and run some errands.

"Mrs. Murphy," Burke said.

"Oh, please, you old fool," Kai said.

"Do you prefer Kai, or do I risk getting shot?" Burke said.

"Come to your point before I lose patience with you and throw you from this wagon," Kai said.

"I've been a good boy for many years," Burke said. "Quite frugal in fact."

"If you mean you never paid a bar tab in your life, I believe you," Kai said.

"My point is this," Burke said. "I have a fair amount of money saved, and I'd like to invest some of it in your whiskey business. I think Tennessee is a fine place to live and by investing, it will give me something to occupy my time."

"Besides drinking it, you mean," Kai said.

"A man needs various interests," Burke said.

"When you say invest, you mean exactly what?" Kai said.

"I was looking things over this morning while you were tending to the baby," Burke said. "It seems to me you will never increase production without expansion. You might get six hundred barrels from your present situation, but if a second distillery was built on Murphy's land, you could double it."

Kai looked at Burke. "And you'd willing to invest in a second distillery?"

"What do you think I've been talking about?" Burke said.

"You'll need to discuss it with Murphy when he returns," Kai said.

"I know that," Burke said. "I'm looking for your blessing."

They reached the post office and Kai stepped down. "I'll only be a minute," she said.

Burke lit a cigar while Kai entered the post office. She returned with a stack of mail and climbed back into the wagon.

"A telegram from Murphy and from Harry," Kai said. She opened Murphy's first. "He is in Carson City. He said he wrote a letter." Then she opened Harry's telegram. "He said he had excellent results and will be returning in three days for a short rest."

"Harry, huh?" Burke said.

Sometimes Boyle just wanted to run. Part Belgian Draft, Boyle was incredibly large and powerful, but he also had tremendous stamina and enjoyed showing it off to Murphy.

Murphy let him go for five miles, then eased Boyle into a trot, a walk, and finally they stopped beside the Carson River.

Murphy removed the saddle and gave Boyle a quick brushing, then let him roam a bit to eat sweet grass.

Then Murphy lit his pipe, sat against a tree, and watched the Carson River, so named for the great frontiersman Kit Carson. Murphy would have liked to have known Carson, but the man died in sixty-eight while Murphy was still in Grant's army, working as railroad police chief during the expansion.

Once Boyle had his belly full of grass, he wandered over to Murphy. "Ready to retire, boy?" Murphy said. "Think of all those colts and fillies you can sire."

Boyle looked at Murphy.

"You're fifteen now, boy," Murphy said. "Hell, you'll make it to thirty-five, easy. Hell, you'll outlive me."

Boyle snorted.

"You're right, we should get back," Murphy said and stood up.

"How are you feeling, Johnson?" Murphy said.

"Not so poorly, no thanks to you," Johnson said.

Murphy and Hale were in Johnson's room in the doctor's office. Johnson's right ankle was still chained to the brass bedrail.

"The doctor said you can travel tomorrow," Murphy said.

"Bully for the doc," Johnson said.

"Not so bully for you, kid," Murphy said. "You get a one-way ride to a hanging party where you're the star."

"Don't take offense if I disagree," Johnson said.

"You know what's a shame, Johnson?" Murphy said. "Having your life snuffed out at the age of twenty-three. Twenty-three years just doesn't seem enough."

"You're just trying to scare me," Johnson said. "It won't work."

"No?" Murphy said.

"No," Johnson said.

Murphy took a pencil out of a pocket and his penknife. With the penknife he whittled away at the wood of the pencil.

"What the hell are you doing?" Johnson said.

"Yeah, what are you doing?" Hale said.

When the lead was fully exposed, Murphy removed a card from his jacket pocket and shaved the lead onto the card in a pile.

"Give me your right thumb," Murphy said.

"What for?" Johnson said.

"Because if you don't, I'll break it," Murphy said.

"Sheriff?" Johnson said.

"I'd give him your thumb, kid," Hale said.

Johnson held out his thumb. Murphy set the card on the

small table beside the bed and then pressed Johnson's thumb into the pile of lead shavings.

Murphy then lifted the card and blew on it until all that remained was Johnson's thumbprint in the lead. "See that, kid? That's your thumbprint," Murphy said.

"So?" Johnson said.

"Fingerprints are like snowflakes," Murphy said. "No two are alike. Point is, every time I look at this card, I'll think of you and how you died young and stupid."

Murphy nodded and then walked out of the room.

"Hey," Johnson shouted. "You think I want to die? You think I want to hang? Are you crazy?"

"Good night, Johnson," Hale said.

Murphy and Hale stopped by the Carson Saloon for a quick drink after leaving Johnson.

"Can I see that card?" Hale said.

Murphy took the card out of a pocket and handed it to Hale.

"Is that true what you said about fingerprints?" Hale said.

"Completely," Murphy said. "Every man's fingers leave their own mark. Someday soon, fingerprints will catch more criminals and outlaws than any posse ever could."

"Something you learned in the secret service?" Hale said.

"Among other things," Murphy said.

"What time does your train leave?" Hale said.

"Ten o'clock."

"I'll see you off," Hale said.

CHAPTER FORTY-SEVEN

Kai, Burke, and the foreman took the wagon across the stream to Murphy's farmhouse.

"Where the barn is now can be converted to a distillery. A warehouse to hold the barrels can be built right behind it," Burke said. "You can double production the first year and sell twice as much within three years."

"My husband would have to approve," Kai said.

"Why wouldn't he if I pay half the cost?" Burke said. "Double production at half the expense. You'd need another drummer like Harry, maybe even two, but think of the potential for the future."

"What I'm thinking of is occupying Murphy's time enough so he's too busy to go around the country chasing outlaws," Kai said. "And I have the feeling you're thinking the same thing."

"You're a smart woman, Kai," Burke said.

"And don't you forget it, Burke," Kai said.

Johnson was placed in shackled handcuffs. The shackles went around his waist and the handcuffs were attached to the shackles, limiting his ability to move or use his arms.

"This ain't fair," Johnson said. "You got me hog-tied like I was some animal."

"Kid, we'll be on this train for about thirty hours," Murphy said. "You can spend the ride in a sleeping car or in the boxcar with my horse. It depends on how much you annoy me."

211

"Have a safe trip, Murphy," Hale said. "And let me know the outcome."

Murphy and Hale shook hands. Then Murphy and Johnson got aboard the train. Murphy took Johnson to their double sleeping car.

"Pick a bed, kid, and make yourself comfortable," Murphy said as he tossed his bag and saddlebags in the corner.

"How can I get comfortable tied up like some hog?" Johnson said.

"You made your bed, kid," Murphy said. "I offered you a chance, and you sided with Holland and Moats. It's time you learned to take responsibility for your own actions."

Johnson flopped on a bed. "What do you know about it?" he said.

"I know you come from a good family," Murphy said. "And even if you didn't want to be a farmer, you were a fair hand at cowboying."

"With somebody else's cows," Johnson said. "Working for thirty a month and a cot. That ain't no kind of life for a man."

"And you think being dropped from a scaffold and having your neck broken like a dry chicken bone is?" Murphy said. "And while you swing, Holland and Moats are out there having a fine time with all that money. Face it, kid. You're nothing to them. And I'll tell you something else. It's always somebody else's cows. Nothing is ever really owned, kid. Just borrowed. Even the air you breathe."

"Shut up," Johnson said. "I don't want to talk no more."

"Suit yourself," Murphy said.

Murphy removed his jacket and tossed it on his bed. Then he opened his suitcase and took out a book, lit his pipe, and sat in the chair to read.

"I was denied breakfast this morning," Johnson said. "Even a prisoner gets to eat three times a day."

"I'll order lunch at noon," Murphy said. "Now be quiet."

"What am I supposed to do for the next thirty hours?" Johnson said.

"I have an extra book," Murphy said.

"A book?" Johnson said.

"We can talk if you'd rather," Murphy said.

"Screw you," Johnson said.

"Ever see a man hang, kid?" Murphy said. "You drop through that trapdoor and the sound is like no other. Sometimes you dangle for a long time as the rope chokes the life out of you. Most wet and soil their pants. At the end, you twitch and jerk and finally you go still. It's not pretty to behold. That's what's waiting for you when we get off this train, kid."

Johnson stared at Murphy. "You're just trying to scare me, is what you're doing," he said.

"I am scaring you, and you'll be scared a lot worse when we reach Fort Smith," Murphy said. "I never met a tough guy yet who didn't whimper and cry for his mama when it came time to take that final walk."

"You just shut your mouth," Johnson said.

"Sure, kid," Murphy said. "What would you like for lunch?"

Burke and Kai poured over the paperwork on the desk in Michael's den.

"I have to admit this Harry fellow knows how to sell," Burke said. "The orders are flowing in like water."

"If we expand as you suggest, we'll need more than one Harry," Kai said.

"When did he say he'd be back?" Burke said.

"Day after tomorrow," Kai said.

"I'd bet he knows other drummers we could employ," Burke said.

"We should meet him at the station when his train arrives," Kai said.

Burke nodded. "I wonder if this is what Murphy had in mind when he brought Harry in and left you to run things?" he said.

Aideen stuck her head into the den. "Lunch," she said.

Before allowing Johnson to eat, Murphy chained his right leg to the iron bedpost and then released his hands.

Lunch was steak with potatoes and carrots and coffee. Murphy ate at the small table and read his book.

Johnson ate quickly. Murphy took his time.

Afterward, Murphy cuffed Johnson's hands again and left his leg chained to the bed.

"What about my leg?" Johnson said.

"I'm going to leave that on for a while," Murphy said. "I believe I'll have a nap."

"A nap?" Johnson said. "How can you have a nap with me hog-tied like this?"

"Clear conscience, kid," Murphy said. "Makes for easy sleeping."

CHAPTER FORTY-EIGHT

At a layover stop, Murphy left Johnson chained to the bed and went to the boxcar to visit Boyle. There was enough time for a quick brushing and to feed him a few carrot sticks before the train left the station.

When Murphy returned to the sleeping car, Johnson was asleep.

He sat at the small table, lit his pipe, and wrote a letter to Kai. Johnson rolled in his sleep, and the chains rattled.

Murphy looked over at Johnson as he moaned in his sleep, screamed, and bolted awake.

"Dreaming about the gallows, kid?" Murphy said.

"You rot in hell," Johnson said.

"Save me a seat," Murphy said. "I figure I'll be along twenty or so years after you."

"I ain't hung yet, you murderous undertaker," Johnson said.

"Your undoing is of your own accord, Johnson," Murphy said. "I extended you the olive branch, and you chose to spit in my face. I had my way, I'd pull the lever myself."

Johnson glared at Murphy. "I could kill you," he said.

"You had your chance," Murphy said. "You won't get another one."

Kai held the baby after a midnight feeding and walked around the living room. She turned and looked at Burke in his nightshirt, lantern in hand as he quietly strolled in.

"I thought I heard a noise," Burke said.

"I'm sorry if I woke you," Kai said.

"I was awake," Burke said. "I rarely go to bed early."

Kai sat on the sofa and Burke sat next to her. "May I?" Burke said.

Kai handed him the baby and he placed her head on his right shoulder.

"If the Washington elite could see you now," Kai said.

"I imagine it must be quite the sight to see Murphy holding her and giving her a bottle," Burke said.

"To tell you the truth, he's terrified to hold her," Kai said. "He acts like she's going to break apart in his hands."

Burke returned the baby to Kai. "Put the little one to bed and get some sleep," he said.

Murphy kept a lantern on the table lit on low flame so there was enough light for him to see Johnson.

Johnson tossed and turned as he slept. His face was a sheen of sweat. He was breaking down.

He would fall apart once in front of Judge Parker.

The question unanswered was: did he have anything to give up?

Suddenly Johnson screamed, "No!" opened his eyes, and sat up in his bed.

"Did you hear those gallows snap again, kid?" Murphy said. "We'll be in Fort Smith tomorrow, Johnson. Best get some sleep."

CHAPTER FORTY-NINE

Murphy walked Boyle and Johnson from the railroad station to Judge Parker's courthouse. After securing Johnson in a holding cell, Murphy entered the courthouse and went to Parker's chambers.

"What happened to your head?" Parker said as he poured two shots of bourbon.

"Johnson bushwhacked me on the way to Carson City," Murphy said.

"From the looks of it, you're lucky to be alive," Parker said.

"I thought he was salvageable," Murphy said. "He isn't. That's a mistake I won't make twice."

"Have him in my courtroom tomorrow at ten," Parker said. "If he needs it, get him shaved and bathed."

"He needs it," Murphy said.

"Will you stay in town tonight?" Parker said.

Murphy nodded.

"Get yourself settled, and we'll have dinner tonight," Parker said.

Kai and Burke greeted Harry as he stepped off the train.

"Harry, this is an old friend, Mr. William Burke," Kai said.

Harry and Burke shook hands.

"You're quite a salesman, judging by the orders you filled," Burke said.

"It's not difficult when you're selling a good product," Harry said. "Of course, you have to display a certain amount of flamboyance to get your point across, but it comes down to product."

"A bit of panache never hurts," Burke said.

"Did you dine on the train?" Kai said.

"I did not," Harry said.

"Shall we go to Delmonico's?" Kai said.

In the lobby, Murphy met Marshals Cal Whitson and Bass Reeves.

"Your head?" Whitson said.

"That man I just brought in, he bushwhacked me on the trail," Murphy said. "He's scheduled for Parker's court tomorrow at ten. Do me a favor and have the guards get him cleaned up before court."

"We'll pass it along," Whitson said. "Are you headed home?"

"I'm staying in town tonight," Murphy said. "Having dinner with the judge. Why don't you join us at seven at my hotel."

"We'll be there," Reeves said.

Burke, Kai, and Harry took a window table at Delmonico's Restaurant.

"Harry, Kai, and I have been discussing the idea of expanding the business," Burke said. "Doubling the barrel production is the goal."

"I can barely keep up with the orders now," Harry said. "We'd need more drummers to fill the orders and expand the territory."

"And that's where you come in, Harry," Burke said. "You must know dozens of qualified drummers who would like to get in on a ground-floor opportunity."

"As a matter of fact, I do," Harry said.

"Excellent," Burke said. "Shall we order?"

Murphy treated Parker, Whitson, and Reeves to the best steak the Fort Smith Steakhouse offered. Although Arkansas had sided with the south during the war, ten percent of the population consisted of freed slaves. Bass Reeves, once a slave himself, was welcome and respected everywhere.

"Bass, Cal, I want you to escort this Johnson kid to court at ten o'clock tomorrow morning," Parker said. "As Murphy is the one bringing charges and will take the witness stand, I don't want him transporting the prisoner."

"No problem, Judge," Whitson said.

"The old gallows. I want men working on it at sunup, so he can see it from his cell," Parker said. "Give him something to think about."

Whitson and Reeves grinned.

"Dead man's walk gets them every time," Reeves said.

"We'll have a drink after dinner and toast to a successful outcome," Parker said.

Chapter Fifty

Harry looked at Burke's rough sketches of the new distillery that would be located behind the storage warehouse on Murphy's farm across the river.

"Michael Murphy was convinced it was the fresh water from the creek and the homegrown corn that made his bourbon exceptional whiskey, and I agree with him," Burke said. "And the second distillery would have use of the same water and corn."

Harry nodded. "I would need at least two drummers to supervise, but once territories were established, the product will sell itself," he said.

"I'm very excited about this, Harry," Burke said. "It's an undertaking that would honor the memory of Michael Murphy, as well as secure our niche in the business."

"Understandable, but I wonder what Mr. Murphy will have to say about all this," Harry said.

"Harry, why do you think he sent you to us?" Burke said. "Now let's go to breakfast before the women get their dander up."

Johnson awoke to the sound of the gallows' trapdoor springing open and a sandbag dropping.

He stood on his bunk and watched as two men reset the trapdoor and dropped another sandbag.

The noise made him sick to his stomach. He had to empty

220

his bladder and jumped down to grab the large basin in the corner.

A bit later, two marshals came to get him.

"Let's go, Johnson," the black marshal said. "The judge wants you shaved and clean for his courtroom."

They took him to a barber in the lobby of the courthouse for a shave and haircut, then to the bathing room where prisoners were allowed one bath a week.

Then, at five minutes to ten o'clock, Johnson was escorted into the courtroom and placed at a table where he sat alone.

Except for the two marshals, the courtroom was empty.

At ten o'clock, Murphy walked in and sat at the table on the other side of the courtroom. He didn't say anything or look at Johnson.

Everybody sat in silence and waited. Ten long minutes passed, during which time Johnson began to sweat through his shirt.

Then the door to Parker's chambers opened and the judge entered the courtroom.

"All rise," Whitson said.

Murphy, Whitson, Reeves, and Johnson stood. Parker got behind his bench and said, "Be seated," and they all sat.

Parker looked at Johnson. "Young man, you are in serious trouble," he said. "I have studied all the evidence against you and read the reports from Agent Murphy and the sheriffs from Reno and Carson City. Because of the seriousness of your crimes, including the attempted murder of a federal agent, I have no choice but to sentence you to hang. Sentence to be carried out immediately. Take him away."

Johnson jumped to his feet. "What?" he shouted. "I get no trial, no jury, not even a lawyer?"

"I decide what you get," Parker said. "Marshals, take him away and hang him."

that you'll retire," Parker said.

"A team of Clydesdales couldn't get me away from her after this," Murphy said.

Parker nodded. "If you break your word, I'll have you locked up myself," he said.

"If I break my word, throw away the key," Murphy said.

"Let's have dinner tonight at seven," Parker said.

"I won't be good company," Murphy said.

"But I will," Parker said.

Kai, Burke, Harry, and Aideen took coffee on the porch after supper. The baby was asleep on Harry's lap.

"When my son returns, we'll begin the expansion of the new distillery," Aideen said. "You all honor the memory of my late Michael."

Kai took Aideen's hand and gave it a gentle squeeze.

"We'll go to town tomorrow and see if there is some news from Murphy," Kai said.

"I wish you'd allow me to send Reeves and Whitson with you tomorrow," Parker said.

"They would have no jurisdiction outside of Arkansas," Murphy said. "And I've never known you to worry so much about my skin before."

"Goddamn it, Murphy," Parker said. "It's not your skin I'm worried about. I want to try and hang these two in my court, and I can't try and hang dead men."

"I make no promises, but I will do my best to see them to your courtroom alive," Murphy said.

"I will accept that," Parker said.

Finished with dinner at Delmonico's, Murphy and Parker walked to the bar at Murphy's hotel. Murphy ordered two glasses of bourbon.

"I want to see Johnson in the morning before I leave," Murphy said.

"All right, I'll arrange for it," Parker said.

"Thank you, Judge," Murphy said. "And now I'm going to turn in and get some sleep."

For the longest time, probably since he'd met Kai, Murphy hadn't been haunted with dreams and thoughts of the men he killed in battle, with the railroad, and in the secret service.

With the lust for revenge in his heart thirsting like a man lost in a desert would for water, the thoughts and memories returned, vivid and intact.

Murphy sat with his pipe and a glass of bourbon in the hotel room chair and saw the faces of all the men he killed in battle. Some were too old to be soldiers, others were just boys. Yet they refused to surrender, and he wasn't about to let them kill him.

It was war, but the faces and their screams still haunted him.

After the war, when he returned home and discovered that his wife and young child had been murdered by Confederate raiders, he carried that guilt around like a bag of bricks for many years.

Grant saved him by calling him back to service to take part in railroad construction. Murphy headed up the railroad police assigned to protect the project.

The biggest threat came from Native Americans who didn't want the Iron Horse destroying land that was rightfully theirs. Along the way to Utah, especially in the area where Cheyenne, Wyoming, now exists, many Native Americans attacked and died protecting what they believed was their land.

The same thing happened in Utah where the railroads connected.

Murphy had returned to Tennessee, but not for long. Grant was elected president, and he called Murphy to Washington to help with the creation of his secret service. Fifteen years later, he was still serving presidents and doing their bidding.

Then, a few years back, while working for Garfield, he was sent west, where the railroad was expanding again, to stop a madman who was killing railroad workers. He met and fell for Sally Orr, a tough-talking madam, and he brought her home to Tennessee. They were to be married.

Then Garfield called him away on another assignment. While he was gone, Sally was raped and murdered by a carriage driver named Christopher. Murphy blamed himself for not being home.

He searched for Christopher in vain and carried that guilt on his back until he met Kai while on another assignment.

She'd healed his heart after the death of his wife years ago and then his girlfriend Sally Orr, and now that they were married with a new baby, the past could rest.

There was no way on earth he was going to allow any harm to come to her, his mother, and the baby.

Not as long as he drew breath.

The guilt was replaced by anger, and then fury.

And he went to bed and allowed his fury to fester into rage.

CHAPTER FIFTY-TWO

Johnson's left eye was swollen shut. His mouth was a puffy mess, and several of his front teeth were missing. His nose was broken and flat.

He looked at Murphy through his right eye. "I'll be drinking my meals for a month, but the dentist is making me four new front teeth, so I should be on solid food by the time I'm discharged," he said. "And sent to prison," he added.

"You knew they murdered my father, and yet you went along with their scheme to go back and rob my family again," Murphy said. "Why?"

"You got so much, and I got nothing," Johnson said. "It was a chance to get our ranch. It was nothing personal against you and yours."

"If anything happens to my family, when you get out in five years, I will be there," Murphy said. "And I will kill you. You see, to me this is very personal."

Burke drove Kai to town in the buggy. The first stop was at the post office for mail. Mixed in with the regular mail was a telegram from Murphy. She returned to the buggy, sat beside Burke, and opened the telegram.

As she read, Kai's face drained of all color. "Oh, dear God," she said.

"What?" Burke said.

She handed the telegram to Burke. He read it quickly and

227

then snapped the reins.

"We have to get you home right away," he said.

Murphy put Boyle in the boxcar and then shook hands with Parker before boarding the train.

"Good luck," Parker said. "And for God's sake, don't get yourself killed."

Murphy nodded. "Judge," he said and got aboard.

The train left Fort Smith at five minutes past ten in the morning.

"Aideen," Kai shouted as she rushed into the house.

"The bedroom," Aideen said.

Kai rushed to the bedroom. Aideen was on her bed with the baby, who was asleep.

"Gather the baby's things and some for yourself," Kai said.

"What's happened?" Aideen said.

Kai showed her the telegram. Aideen glared at Kai. "I'll be damned if they'll run me out of my own home," she said.

"We have the child to think about," Kai said.

"Kai, Aideen, where are you?" Burke called out.

"We'll be right there," Kai said.

Aideen picked up the baby, then she and Kai went to the living room where Burke and the foreman waited.

The foreman looked at Aideen and Kai. "If you'll pardon my speaking out of turn, all the men and I will stay, arm ourselves, and fight those bastards when they arrive," he said.

Kai looked at Burke and he nodded.

Aideen said, "I'll show you Michael's gun safe."

Murphy watched the scenery roll by outside his window at fifty miles per hour. At a bit past noon, he was halfway to Tennessee. The trip on horseback would have taken a week, but by train it was just six hours.

He lit his pipe and continued to watch the scenery. A water stop was coming up shortly. He could feel the train start to lose speed.

At the water stop, Murphy stood and exited the train to stretch his back. The process of taking on water and coal usually took about fifteen minutes. He watched as the water chute and coal chute were put in place and their loads were dumped.

Even twenty years ago, most people hadn't ridden a train. Today riding trains was commonplace.

The country was shrinking.

But that didn't make it civilized.

Harry was in the distillery when the men stopped working and started to file out.

"What's happening?" Harry said.

"Trouble," a worker said.

Harry joined the four men from the distillery and another four from the warehouse as they walked to the house.

When they reached the house, Burke and the foreman were standing on the porch.

"Men, this is Mr. Burke," the foreman said. "He'd like a few words with you."

Burke stepped forward and held up a telegram. "Men, this is a telegram from Murphy," he said. "It says the men who robbed and murdered Michael are on their way back to rob the place again."

The men immediately started to buzz.

"Now hold on a moment," Burke said. "The telegram also says Murphy will be here later this afternoon. I, for one, will not allow him to face those men alone, bushwhackers that they are. Any man who wants to help Murphy fight those men, step forward."

The first man forward was Harry.

Then everybody else followed.

"Good lads," Burke said. "If you haven't a weapon of your own, Michael has a well-stocked gun safe."

At four o'clock, the train rolled to a stop in the station. Murphy stepped out onto the platform and walked to the boxcar.

Boyle was anxious and antsy when Murphy put the saddle on him.

"You want to run?" Murphy said as he guided Boyle out of the boxcar to the platform and then to the road.

Murphy mounted the saddle and rubbed Boyle's massive neck.

"Now show me something," Murphy said and yanked the reins.

CHAPTER FIFTY-THREE

When Murphy slowed Boyle to a walk and passed through the gate, he was surprised to find Burke and Harry sitting on the porch with shotguns on their laps and glasses of lemonade in their hands.

Murphy dismounted without tying Boyle to the hitching post.

"What in the world?" Murphy said.

He climbed up to the porch and looked at Burke and Harry. "Are those my father's Greeners?" Murphy said.

Burke patted the shotgun on his lap. "They are," he said. "And fine weapons at that."

"Harry, that shotgun is bigger than you," Murphy said.

"I can handle it," Harry said.

The door opened and Kai stepped out, wearing a holster and six-gun around her waist. "Welcome home, my husband," she said.

"Welcome home? Have you . . ." Murphy said.

Aideen came out to the porch and she, too, was wearing a holster and six-gun.

"Mother?" Murphy said.

Aideen reached up to kiss Murphy's cheek. "Good to have you home, son," she said. "Supper is almost ready. Come in and wash up and join the boys."

"What boys? Has everybody lost their minds?" Murphy said.

Kai smiled at Murphy. "These men, they worked for and loved your father," she said. "They are not about to let the two men who murdered him get away a second time."

Murphy sighed. "Marvelous," he said.

After supper, Murphy took the men to the porch.

"I know and appreciate how all of you felt about my father," he said. "And that you've taken up arms to protect his wife and property tells me all I need to know about your feelings and the kind of men you are, but I must ask you this."

The men looked at Murphy and waited.

"Have any of you ever killed a man?" Murphy said. "If you have, step forward."

Nobody moved.

"I ran over a dog with a buggy once," Harry said. "It was unintentional, of course, the poor fellow."

Murphy looked at Harry and sighed. "When you kill a man, it's like putting a small hole in your soul," he said. "It stays with you for the rest of your days. Even if it was totally justified and necessary, that hole will never be filled in again. And the more you kill, the bigger that hole becomes. I just want you to understand that before you pull a trigger with the purpose of taking a life."

The foreman stepped forward. "I believe I speak for every man here when I say I have no desire to kill, but those men took the life of a man we all loved, so I am willing to do whatever is necessary to see justice done," he said.

"You all feel that way?" Murphy said.

"They all do," Burke said.

"If you mean what you say, then you'll listen to what I say and do what I say when I say it," Murphy said. "Agreed?"

"You're the law, Mr. Murphy," the foreman said. "We'll do everything you say."

"Those men won't return during the day," Murphy said. "They will strike in the darkness of early morning to take us by surprise. In our sleep is when we're at our weakest. So we will be ready for them to call on us at night."

"When will they be here?" Burke said.

"If my calculations based upon the timetable I was given are correct, in two or three nights," Murphy said. "We have much to work out, and I suggest we do that over coffee and the cake the ladies have baked for us."

After the foreman and crew went home for the evening, Murphy and Burke sat in chairs on the porch with small glasses of whiskey.

Burke smoked a cigar, Murphy his pipe.

"So what are you going to do to keep these good but misguided souls from getting killed?" Burke said.

"Whatever I can," Murphy said.

"I imagine Cleveland is asking Arthur why you're not available for his second tour," Burke said.

"Cleveland thinks the west has settled and is refined," Murphy said. "Tell him to go stump in McAllister for some up-close refinement."

Burke blew a smoke ring and grinned. "Tomorrow let's talk about expanding the whiskey business," he said.

"Tomorrow," Murphy said. "Right now I need some sleep."

As Kai brushed her hair, she watched Murphy in her dresser mirror. He had a bruise on the left side of his forehead, and he winced slightly when he removed his shirt. She saw the new scar on the left side of his chest where a bullet had probably broken a rib.

Kai stood and removed her robe. "Have you the strength for what I have in mind to do to you?" she said.

"It will probably kill me, but I can think of no better way to go," Murphy said.

Kai kissed the bruised rib. "Come to bed," she said.

CHAPTER FIFTY-FOUR

After breakfast, Murphy, Burke, and Harry went to Michael's den where Burke and Harry had prepared charts, diagrams, and estimates for Murphy to review.

"You did some selling," Murphy said to Harry.

"And I'll do better when I go out again," Harry said.

"I want you to hit Reno, but I'll be going with you," Murphy said. "They have more saloons and gambling halls than any town I've ever been in, but it's a wild place for a stranger. Once you're established I think you will be all right there."

"What do you think of the sketches for the new distillery and warehouse on your property?" Burke said.

"Let's take a ride over and do some measuring," Murphy said. "See if we can figure out the costs."

"Twenty thousand for distillery and warehouse is my guess, of which I'll invest half," Burke said.

"So you're serious about retirement and relocating?" Murphy said.

"It's time," Burke said. "For both of us."

"We need another drummer, maybe two," Harry said.

Murphy nodded. "There is an architect in town," he said. "We can engage him to design what we need. But first, let's take a ride."

Murphy, Burke, and Harry walked through the barn on Murphy's property.

"If we open up the roof and add tiers, we can have room for four hundred barrels," Burke said. "We can build the distillery close to the creek and take advantage of the same fresh mountain water as your father. You grow enough corn for six hundred barrels a year."

Murphy looked at Harry.

"It can be done," Harry said. "And I can sell it."

"We need to discuss living arrangements," Murphy said. "Over lunch."

"Now that you've brought it up, it only makes sense for Mr. Burke and Harry to occupy my house while I go across the creek and live with you," Aideen said to Murphy and Kai. "If I wouldn't be in the way."

"Mother," Murphy said.

"You'd no more be in the way than the baby," Kai said.

"It's settled then," Murphy said.

The foreman and workers had supper at the house, then divided up into shifts for the night.

Murphy and Burke went to the corral where Murphy would sleep with Boyle.

"A nightcap for the cold air," Burke suggested and produced a flask.

"The barometer on the tree says it's seventy-three degrees," Murphy said.

"Then a nightcap to fight the heat," Burke said. He took a sip and passed the flask to Murphy.

Murphy took a sip and returned the flask.

"What if you fall asleep?" Burke said.

"I intend to sleep," Murphy said. "Anybody gets close to the house, Boyle will wake me up."

"I've never committed a violent act in my life," Burke said.

"And you won't be committing one now," Murphy said. "This is my kind of game, remember?"

Burke nodded. "Kai will be wanting to say good night."

Burke left the corral and entered the house. Murphy lit his pipe and sat against Boyle's saddle. Boyle looked at him.

"I don't want to be penned in here any more than you do," Murphy said.

Kai came out carrying a tray and walked to the corral. Murphy stood and opened the gate.

"I brought you a pot of coffee, a glass of milk, and some apple pie," she said.

Murphy took the tray and set it beside the saddle.

"I should be sleeping here with you," Kai said.

"Don't be ridiculous," Murphy said.

"What is ridiculous about a woman sleeping with her husband?" Kai said.

"In a corral?" Murphy said.

"I slept on hard, frozen ground with the Sioux and Navajo for years," Kai said. "I can certainly spend the night in a corral."

"But you won't," Murphy said.

"No, I won't," Kai said.

Kai kissed Murphy good night and returned to the house.

Around one in the morning, Murphy stretched out in his bedroll. "Give me a nudge if anybody shows up," he told Boyle.

CHAPTER FIFTY-FIVE

"It's been two nights now," Burke said. "My nerves can't take much more of this. Why not get the sheriff in town and send for some marshals?"

"This is my kind of game, Burke," Murphy said. "You and everybody else can cross the creek and stay in my house if it will ease your nerves."

Murphy and Burke were having coffee on the porch after breakfast.

"No. We'll stay," Burke said. "But those men better show pretty soon, or I'll wind up in a sanatorium."

"You need something to occupy your mind," Murphy said.

"Such as?"

Murphy, Burke, and Harry spent the morning on the side of the barn, chopping wood, although Murphy did most of the chopping.

"I never knew chopping wood was so rough on the hands," Harry said.

"And the back," Burke said.

"Want to quit?" Murphy said.

"Actually, I'm rather enjoying this," Harry said.

"Burke?" Murphy said.

"Like you said, my mind is now occupied," Burke said. "With how much my back hurts."

★ ★ ★ ★ ★

Kai brought Murphy a cup of coffee on the porch.

"The both of them are soaking in tubs of hot water with salts," Kai said. "I had to fix the blisters on their hands."

"A little hard work won't kill them," Murphy said.

"I'm not so sure about that," Kai said.

The foreman approached the porch. "We're ready to rotate barrels," he said. "Would you pick out the ones you want moved?"

Murphy stood. "I can do better than that," he said.

Kai took the chair while Murphy walked off with the foreman. A few minutes later, Burke appeared on the porch.

"Where's Murphy?" he said.

"Rotating barrels," Kai said. "Want to give him a hand?"

"I think I'll stick to just drinking the stuff," Burke said. "It's easier on the back."

of the man.

Kai watched, frozen in place. She knew that Murphy was capable of great feats of violence, but not to the extent she was witnessing.

Burke ran to Murphy's side.

"Murphy, that's enough," Burke said. "We need them alive."

Murphy didn't hear him or chose to ignore him. Kai ran from the corral to Murphy's side.

"Don't kill him," Kai said. "Please don't kill him."

Murphy looked at Kai and released his hands from Moats's throat.

Kai extended her hand. Murphy took it, and Kai led him into the house. Aideen followed them and closed the door.

"All right men, let's tie these two up," Burke said. "What's left of them."

CHAPTER FIFTY-SEVEN

Murphy, Kai, Aideen, Burke, and Harry occupied the first pew in Judge Parker's courtroom.

The mood was somber. The courtroom was as quiet as an empty church.

Harry cleared his throat, and the sound echoed slightly.

The side door opened and Cal Whitson and Bass Reeves escorted Moats and Holland into the courtroom. The shackles on Moats and Holland clanked and echoed loudly.

"Sit down," Whitson said.

Moats and Holland took chairs at the defense table.

Whitson walked across the floor to Murphy. "This telegram from Grover Cleveland came for you in care of the court," he said.

Murphy took the envelope, removed the telegram, and read it quickly. Then he looked at Kai and tore it up. She nodded her approval.

A moment later, Judge Parker entered the courtroom.

"All rise," Whitson said.

ABOUT THE AUTHOR

Al Lamanda, writing as Ethan J. Wolfe, is the author of twenty western novels, including The Regulator series, The Youngblood Brothers series, and The Illinois Detective Agency series.

The employees of Five Star Publishing hope you have enjoyed this book.

Our Five Star novels explore little-known chapters from America's history, stories told from unique perspectives that will entertain a broad range of readers.

Other Five Star books are available at your local library, bookstore, all major book distributors, and directly from Five Star/Gale.

Connect with Five Star Publishing

Website:
  gale.com/five-star

Facebook:
  facebook.com/FiveStarCengage

Twitter:
  twitter.com/FiveStarCengage

Email:
  FiveStar@cengage.com

For information about titles and placing orders:
  (800) 223-1244
  gale.orders@cengage.com

To share your comments, write to us:
  Five Star Publishing
  Attn: Publisher
  10 Water St., Suite 310
  Waterville, ME 04901